It's going to be an interesting year...

It was Beth Patterson's first day back at school and she was busy stuffing things in her locker.

"Beth, I've been looking for you," said a male voice from behind her.

"Hi, Adam," said Beth, recognizing her friend's voice without bothering to turn around. "Sorry I forgot to call you back last night."

Suddenly the hallway seemed hushed. The girls stopped their chatter, and Beth turned around to see what was going on.

She was in for the surprise of her life. Adam Brainard—good old friendly Adam, her pal since second grade, the one boy she had just sworn she could never have a crush on—was suddenly six-foot-four and *gorgeous!*

HAMPSTEAD HIGH

Only Friends

by
Betsy Harris

Troll Associates

Library of Congress Cataloging-in-Publication Data

Harris, Betsy.
    Only friends.

    (Hampstead High; 3)
    Summary: When Beth sees her old pal Adam for the first
time since he went to summer camp, she is so struck by
the changes in him she knows they can no longer be
"only friends."
    [1. High schools—Fiction.   2. Schools—Fiction]
I. Title.   II. Series: Harris, Betsy.   Hampstead
High; 3.
PZ7.H2409On 1991   [Fic]   89-20371
ISBN 0-8167-1012-8

A TROLL BOOK, published by Troll Associates

Only Friends

Chapter One

"Isn't that the new guy from Mayview?" whispered Beth Patterson to her best friend, Kate. "He is definitely the cutest thing I've ever seen!"

Kate Morris—blond, beautiful, and brainy— laughed as she answered her friend. "Give me a break, will you? It's only our first day back and already you've picked out the guy of your dreams —at least for today." Kate waved back to a guy who'd almost tripped over himself saying hello. "Why don't you try to settle on one guy for a little longer than twenty-four hours?"

"Easy for *you* to say," replied Beth. "If you even *think* about a guy, he's chasing after you the next minute. Honestly, sometimes I think you have ESP."

"You don't need ESP, Beth. Guys chase after you, too. You just don't notice because you're too busy being madly in love with someone you don't even know."

Beth was pretty, too, but in a different way from Kate. Her dark hair was cut short, and it was the thick, shiny kind that always falls into place perfectly. She was shorter than Kate, with small, delicate features, big gray eyes, and long, curly lashes.

Beth sighed, thinking over what Kate had just said. Then she brightened. "Well, if you help me think of a way to meet 'Mr. Mayview,' then I'll know him, and *then* I'll fall madly in love with him." Beth was only half joking as she pointed out the cute new guy again.

The two girls had just walked in through the large front entrance of the school. It was a beautiful warm September morning, and Beth and Kate were looking forward to the start of the school year. Their schedules were packed with lots of fun activities at Hampstead, like cheerleading, drama club, and the homecoming committee. Kate was sort of a superstar at school, and Beth was popular, too. She was bright and fun, and no one could resist her energy and enthusiasm once she got interested in something. But what Beth was interested in most of the time was BOYS.

"Seriously, don't you ever get tired of talking about guys?" asked Kate as they started walking down the hall toward their lockers. Beth looked at her as if she'd just dropped in from outer space.

"What kind of a question is that?" Beth replied. "That's what guys are *for*."

The girls were jostled and bumped along the school corridor by hundreds of other students. As usual, everyone looked as if they had stepped out of the pages of the latest magazines—or at least had tried to look that way. Beth had on a peach cotton dress that showed off the tan she'd worked on all summer. She had also lost a few pounds and really looked great. Kate was wearing a short white skirt and pale-pink-and-green-striped polo shirt—today she'd gone for a preppy look.

"I mean, they're just people. *Different* people," she grinned. "But haven't you ever just been *friends* with a guy, or do you always have to fall head over heels madly in love, if-you-don't-get-him-you'll-die—"

"Sure I have," said Beth, interrupting Kate in mid-sentence. "Adam Brainard and I have been friends since second grade, and we write to each other every summer. I've *never* had a crush on him. And I bet I never will. You know, it's like—oh, you know, he's practically my brother. I could never have a crush on Adam."

"Beth, you could have a crush on *anybody*. Anyway, what's your first class today?" said Kate.

"English. I've got Mrs. Griffith—I hear she's really great," Beth said hopefully. She'd heard rumors about how hard she was, but she didn't want to believe them.

"Remember, she's supposed to be really tough and she gives a lot of homework," Kate reminded her as she brushed her hair back from her shoulders. Kate always had the inside scoop on everything at school from her older sister, Amy, who'd graduated from Hampstead last spring.

The two girls had reached their lockers—right near each other. The wide corridor was packed with students. As Beth and Kate elbowed a little space for themselves and started cramming their books and other stuff into their lockers, they were surrounded by their friends from the cheerleading squad. The air filled with greetings, giggles, and gossip.

"Hi, Kate!"

"How you doing, Kate? Hi, Beth! How was your summer?"

"Hi, Kate, see you at cheerleading practice this afternoon!"

"Hey, Beth, did you see the new transfer student from Mayview? He's really gorgeous."

"Beth, have you seen Adam Brainard since he got back from that wilderness camp?" asked Cynthia Jones, a cheerleader with long strawberry-blond hair.

"No. He called last night, but I forgot to call him back," answered Beth absently. Right now, she had other things on her mind besides Adam.

"Just wondering," said Cynthia.

"Who've you got for English, Beth?" asked Robin James, one of Kate and Beth's friends.

"Mrs. Griffith," replied Beth.

"Me, too," said Robin with a grimace. "At least we'll have each other to complain to about all that homework."

"Oh no, it's true!" groaned Beth. "I thought for once Kate's sister might be wrong."

The girls gathered together, trading stories and blocking the flow of traffic through the crowded corridor. As the other students slowed down to squeeze by them, different boys stopped to say hi, and see what had happened to the girls during the summer.

Billy Hutton walked by slowly, gazing at Kate. "Hi, Kate," he said dreamily. The girls all said hi, and giggled as he walked down the corridor.

"He always looks like he's going to faint when he's around you, Kate," said Beth, feeling just a little jealous. Billy Hutton had been in love with Kate since ninth grade, and Beth thought he was really neat.

"Take it easy, Beth," said Robin. "I have a feeling this is going to be a good year for you. You look great!"

"Thanks," said Beth as she started loading up her locker: an extra hairbrush, lip gloss, chewing gum, breath mints, a Weird Noise rock poster taped to the inside, and a mirror hanging on the door.

"Beth—I've been looking for you," said a male voice from behind her.

"Hi, Adam," said Beth, recognizing her friend's voice without bothering to turn around. "Sorry I forgot to call you back last night."

Suddenly the hallway seemed hushed. The girls stopped their chatter, and Beth turned around to see what was going on.

She was in for the surprise of her life. Adam Brainard—good old friendly Adam, her pal since second grade, the one boy she had just sworn she could never have a crush on—was suddenly six-foot-four and *gorgeous*!

What had happened to him? Did they give rock-star lessons at that camp he went to? Could a guy really shoot up over four inches in less than four months? And his hair—she didn't remember it looking like this: dark, thick, curly. Was this really Adam, her old friend? Beth shook herself, realizing that she'd been standing there with her mouth open like an idiot. Her friends were beginning to giggle at the whole scene.

"Hi, Beth," said Adam casually. "I don't mind that you didn't call me back last night." He put on a fake, funny-hurt look that Beth had seen hundreds of times, only now it made her feel different. She wanted to reach up and brush any hurt away.

5

"Oh, don't look like that," was all Beth could manage. She was still too stunned by the "new" Adam. She kept telling herself it's just the same old Adam, but her heart wasn't saying that.

"I thought you liked my basset hound imitation," Adam teased, and tousled Beth's hair as he'd done since they were eight years old.

Beth's head was spinning. "How come you...?" she started to ask Adam, but her question was cut off by the 9:00 A.M. bell.

"C'mon, Beth, we'll be late," said Robin. "Mrs. Griffith's class is practically four miles away."

"I'm coming right now," Beth said to Robin as she and Kate dashed down the long corridor. Following behind them, in a graceful, loping run, was Adam Brainard.

"I've got Griffith, too," Adam said as he moved alongside the two girls. "What were you going to ask me, anyway?"

"Oh, nothing, it wasn't important," said Beth. *Oh no,* she thought, *now I haven't even got one period to think this out. Adam Brainard, sexy and gorgeous? What am I going to do? Kate can't be right—she won't be right—I will not have a crush on Adam Brainard...no matter how incredible he looks.*

Kate's sister's advice was on target as usual. Mrs. Griffith's class *was* tough. They were starting the term with poetry, and Beth secretly liked some of the lines of the poems they were reading. Mrs. Griffith had the class take the poetry apart, and put it back together. For most of the period, Beth felt as though *she* was being taken apart—and left that way. Beth couldn't believe it when Adam was called on to read the second poem for the day, a love sonnet. He was only a few seats away from her and she couldn't take her eyes off him as he read. She was barely breathing. *What is happening to me?* she thought.

She wouldn't have too much time to figure any of it out, she realized, as Mrs. Griffith wrote down the titles of three poems—three!—that she expected the class to analyze in writing by Wednesday.

The bell rang, announcing the end of class, and Adam caught up to Beth.

"A lot of work, huh, Beth? But some of those poems were kind of, well...different, not too awful."

Beth remembered a poetry phase Adam had gone through when he was nine. Nothing too wimpy, just some nice rhyming lines about baseball and a sunset. The phase had lasted a couple of weeks. She wished she didn't have so many memories of Adam; it just made the situation harder. Now all she could do was mutter, "Uh, yeah," still not knowing how to react to this gorgeous guy who was "just her friend." "Gotta run. I've got a class over in the science wing. Bye."

What was Beth going to do? She couldn't keep avoiding the new Adam—he really was her friend, after all. But maybe, now, he might become something more; and that made Beth very, very nervous. After all, this wouldn't be just another crush on someone she hardly knew.

The rest of the morning passed in a blur: science class (gross!—they'd probably be dissecting some giant animal, not a tiny frog, this year!); math class (AP math—this terrified most of the kids, but Beth secretly enjoyed the logic of the algebraic manipulations...not that she'd let anyone else know, so she'd said "ugh" along with the rest of the class); and, at last, lunchtime. Maybe she could catch up with Kate or Robin in the cafeteria, and she would be able to talk about her crush on Mike Collins, the captain of the football team, or that cute new transfer from Mayview. Anyone but Adam Brainard.

Beth got to the cafeteria a little late, after stopping to drop off her new textbooks in her locker and check her makeup in the mirror. Kate was already sitting at one of the "in" tables, surrounded by some other cheerleaders and kids from the homecoming committee, with a lot of neat boys stopping by to ask her about her summer. Beth got her lunch and walked over to the table, squeezing herself in between Kate and Robin.

"Wouldn't you know it?" moaned Cynthia Jones. "I've got PE right after lunch! Watch me barf all over my sneakers. And then I have to be sweaty through the rest of my classes—how totally gross!"

"Well, at least you've got a few hours to rest up before cheerleading practice," sighed Robin. "PE's my last class of the day, and then I've got to run and change into my uniform and do somersaults for another two hours!"

"Hi, Beth," said Kate calmly, as if she almost didn't notice the attention from two guys who were passing the table. "How'd your morning go?"

"Great, fine, wonderful. Except your sister was right about Mrs. Griffith. You wouldn't believe the homework. And there was this adorable guy sitting in the front of the class..."

"Is his name Adam Brainard by any chance?" asked Robin mischievously.

"Of course not," replied Beth, slightly flustered that anyone else had noticed the big change in Adam. Even though it was impossible not to notice. "He and I are only friends. No, this guy is really—"

"Didn't look like that to me this morning, in the hallway," continued Robin. "I thought we'd have to wire your jaw shut surgically—it dropped open a mile wide when you turned around and saw him."

"Yeah, well, he *looks* different, that's all. Nothing special," said Beth, trying to act casual. "We're only friends," she repeated trying to convince herself as much as Robin.

"Well, I think he's an absolute HUNK," said Cynthia, giggling a little. "I heard he went to one of those Nature-Bound wilderness camps this summer. They're supposed to make you grow up, or something. Guess it worked—he looks incredible!"

Of course, Beth knew where Adam had been all summer. After all, they'd written to each other. It was just that she'd been picturing someone else in the letters. She shot Cynthia a quick glance—did she really mean it about him being a hunk, or was she just trying to find out how Beth felt? *I can't be jealous,* thought Beth. *Not over Adam Brainard. It's not possible!* She shook her head and made an attempt to start a new conversation.

"Well, we've made it to junior year, but the old 'Hamster High' cafeteria hasn't made it beyond caveman food," Beth said brightly, calling the school by the nickname the kids all used.

"Stop trying to change the subject, Beth," scolded Kate. "Since when don't you want to talk about boys?"

"Me? Are you kidding? It's my favorite topic of conversation," Beth rattled on, doing her best to sound nonchalant. "And I *know* I'm going to get a crush on that new guy from Mayview, Jamie Thompson."

"Yeah," said Kate quietly. "I'm in a couple of classes with him. He's cute, and kind of interesting."

"He was on JV football at Mayview," said Cynthia. "I have a cousin who goes there, and I called her for some info about him. She says he was a real star. I bet he'll go out for the team here, too."

"Great!" said Robin. "I wouldn't mind looking at *him* during cheerleading practice every day!"

Beth breathed a sigh of relief as the conversation turned to Hampstead High's latest arrival. *At least I won't have to see Adam at cheerleading practice*, she thought. *He's never been into football at all. But why am I thinking about Adam again?!*

Lunch went by too fast, and the newly reunited friends once again said their goodbyes, going off to their afternoon classes. Before gym at the end of the day, Beth had history, intermediate Spanish, and her elective course in drama, which she loved.

Beth was surprised to see someone else in her drama class—Adam Brainard. Why was he in all her "emotional" courses, like English and drama, that dealt with love and feelings...where even the simplest poem or monologue seemed to reveal all her hidden emotions?

All kinds of confusing thoughts were spinning around in Beth's head. She realized she was going to have to hide her new feelings so that her friends wouldn't know, and she'd die if Adam knew. This didn't feel like a schoolgirl crush, like the one she'd had on last year's hot rock star, or the captain of the football team, or her older brother's handsome college friends. This was something totally different, and Beth felt as if her breath had been taken away. Every time she looked over at Adam and saw his handsome face, listening to the teacher, reading his book, smiling at her—*smiling at her!*—her heart stopped. What was she going to do?

At last, the bell let Beth out of her drama class— *And out of Adam's sight for the rest of the day,* she thought. Forty-five minutes of running around the gym, and then out to the field for cheerleading practice. *All that exercise will get him out of my head,* Beth decided. And what a break that would be!

Beth and Robin stayed together throughout gym class, and then changed into their cheerleading uniforms.

"Let's hurry up so we can see which guys are going out for the team this year!" Beth said to Robin, making sure she kept her reputation as "the girl who gets crushes on everyone."

"Wait up, you guys. I'm coming too," said Cynthia, suddenly appearing behind them in the locker room.

Robin, Cynthia, and Beth headed out of the school building and onto the practice fields. They wore the school colors, red and white, which clashed with Cynthia's strawberry-blond hair but suited Beth's dark hair and rosy cheeks (rosier now from the time at gym). They started limbering up, trying to look casual as the guys began to run out onto the field.

"Where's that new guy—Jamie?" asked Beth.

"We started talking between classes," said Kate, "and he says he's not going out for football here."

"You're kidding," said Cynthia. "That's kind of weird."

"Maybe," said Kate with a shrug. "He said he's going out for soccer."

"Soccer! That team is so pathetic I can't believe it," said Cynthia, putting her finger down her throat in a mock retch. That was Cynthia's favorite mannerism, one that she used several times a day.

"Checking out the action, girls?" asked a husky male voice from over their shoulders.

Beth was in shock. It was Adam, dressed in a football practice uniform, with a helmet under his arm.

"Not anymore, now that you're here," flirted Cynthia, turning around quickly to grab Adam's attention.

"Yeah, Coach saw me in PE and said I ought to try out for the team. I thought it couldn't hurt. Might even improve my status with the girls, right, Beth?" he said, smiling.

Beth swallowed hard. She had always talked to Adam about how cute the guys on the football team were, how they could take her out any time. She was still reeling a little from Cynthia's blatant flirting with Adam—how could she just act like that, as if he were her best friend? *Wait a minute,* she thought, *this is Adam we're talking about here. Not those other guys you usually get crushes on. Just Adam.*

"Um, sure, I guess so." She swallowed again and blushed even harder. Was this all she was going to be able to say to him ever again? At that moment Beth wished she were Kate—Kate always knew what to say and do, how to act around boys, how to seem cool even when she was nervous and unsure of herself.

"Come on, Adam." Cynthia smiled. "You're not *really* worried about your status with girls...." She looked at him skeptically.

Beth was furious. How could Cynthia come on like that? Then she caught herself. *I'm just like her,* she thought. *I'm always the one fainting over every cute guy, and chasing boys around. I can't do that with Adam. Not Adam! But I don't want her doing it, either. Now what am I supposed to do?*

Beth missed the rest of the conversation between Adam and the other girls. She was too caught up in her own worries.

"Well, I've got to get out onto the field, or the coach'll put me on the bench before I even make the team. Wish me luck."

"Oh, you'll make it, no problem," gushed Cynthia. Beth screwed up her courage. *Where is my usual friendly self?* she wondered. "I know you can do it, pal," she said, finding that she really meant it. "Go for it, Adam."

Adam looked at Beth and smiled. *I think I'm going to melt, right here on the field,* thought Beth.

"Thanks, Beth. You don't know how much that means to me." He ran off with a loping, graceful run—when had he begun to run like that, anyway?—and joined the players assembling on the field.

"Okay, warm-up time," came Kate's voice from behind them.

Beth threw herself into practice, hoping to end the day so exhausted she would just fall into bed and not have to think about her strange new feelings for her old friend Adam Brainard.

Chapter Two

Dear Diary:

Well, the first day of school was really terrific. I can't wait to tell you everything that happened—oh, who am I kidding? I've got to be honest with *you*, Diary. You know I don't want to write about the usual things—cheerleading and drama class and the cute new transfer student...I want to write about Adam Brainard!

Yes, that's right, my old friend Adam. I know, I've hardly mentioned him before, except when I'd ask him stuff about one of the other guys, like Billy Hutton or Mike Collins. But something's happened to him, Diary. He went off to that wilderness camp this summer, and he came back a REAL HUNK!

I've never seen anything like it. I mean, I feel so strange—I wrote him letters during the summer about different guys I had crushes on, and rock stars I wrote to for autographed pictures. I just don't know what to do. I mean, he knows *everything* about me! I can't play hard to get with him, or follow him around, or call him for some dumb reason—I've told him about all those tricks! I've even *asked* him which ones to use on particular guys!

Besides, Diary, something else is going on. I feel...well, *different* about Adam. I mean, it's not like all those other crushes I've told you about. When I look at him, I get this really weird feeling. And when he smiles at me, I just melt inside. And can you believe it, I was actually JEALOUS when Cynthia was flirting with him at football practice (yes, Adam's going out for the team!). I mean, I can almost out-flirt anyone, but not when it comes to Adam.

The worst part is, I can't even talk to my best friend about this. I *swore* to Kate today that I could never have a crush on Adam. And the only other person I could always count on for advice about boys is...guess who? Adam Brainard!

Beth sighed and put down her pen for a moment. *If anyone ever finds this diary and reads it*, she thought, *I'll simply die.* She flipped back through the pages, reading the beginning of a few different entries:

Dear Diary:

Billy Hutton is one of the most FABULOUS boys in school. He is so cute, and funny, and popular. I'll never understand why Kate doesn't snatch him up—he's had a huge crush on her for years. I wish he would pay half as much attention to me. I've tried every trick in the book to get him to notice me more....If I don't make any progress soon, I may have to change my strategy. Any ideas?

Dear Diary:

Weird Noise is the most terrific band I have ever heard. Their music is just AMAZING, their outfits are wild, and their new video is SO HOT. I have a GIGANTIC crush on Rod, the group's gorgeous lead singer. I'm going to write to him, Diary, join his fan club, and travel to all the Weird Noise concerts within a fifty-mile radius of Hampstead. Maybe he'll see me from the stage, and signal to one of his road crew to give me a backstage pass. I know the chances are slim for our meeting, falling in love, and living happily ever after, but I can dream.

* * *

Dear Diary:

Mike Collins, CAPTAIN OF THE FOOTBALL TEAM, actually looked at me today and SMILED. He's only the most incredible guy at Hampstead High, Diary—and he's going to be a senior, too. Can you believe my luck? He noticed me! Now, I've just got to keep his interest. I asked Adam how to make Mike fall in love with me. He told me Mike likes girls who wear short skirts and are really athletic. Time to take up my hems and buy some new sneakers?

Did I write that? wondered Beth. Then, up came another voice from inside her: the old Beth. "Of course you wrote that, silly," said the old Beth. "It's today's entry that was written by some stranger.

What's all this stuff about Adam Brainard? I mean, he looks pretty good and all, but he's just not crush material.''

Beth's first voice returned: *No, really. I feel different about Adam. This isn't just another crush. There's something new going on here. I don't know what it is, but...*

And up came the old Beth again: "How could you know what it is? It's *nothing*, that's what it is! You're just suffering from temporary insanity. I mean, you're not going to tell me you feel 'something special,' are you? That's what you say about *all* your crushes. And besides, what are you going to tell your friends? You're not the kind of girl who gets serious about one guy—you go for them all. Who would believe this? Adam Brainard least of all! He knows your tricks better than anybody.''

Beth shook her head, trying to silence the voices that were plaguing her. She felt as though her head was going to split open from all the confusion inside. "Leave me alone!" she said out loud.

Beth's mother opened the door. "Something wrong, honey?" she asked.

Startled, Beth looked at her mother standing in the doorway. "Oh, no, Mom, I was just, ah, practicing a scene for drama class. Sorry.''

"I know you're in high school," Beth's mother pretended to scold, "and I'm not supposed to be on your case about these things—but don't you think you ought to get some sleep?"

"Okay, Mom, sure. Good night.''

Beth's mother closed the door. Beth looked once more at her diary and shut it with a sigh. Her idea that she would be too tired from gym class and cheerleading practice to think about Adam had fizzled out—even after she had turned out the lights, she kept seeing his handsome face, smiling at her in the darkness of her bedroom.

The next day, Beth woke up feeling like her old self again. She chose a "fun" outfit for school. *This will definitely help me remember the real me*, she thought. *No more of this "true love" nonsense.* She ran downstairs to grab some breakfast before heading off to school. Beth practically skipped down the sidewalk—right there, ahead of her, was Mike Collins, captain of the football team! She jogged up to him.

"Hi, Mike! I'm surprised to see you."

"Oh, hi, Beth. Our car's in the shop being fixed and my ride fell through, so I'm walking for a change." Mike kept walking along as he greeted Beth. He always moved as though he owned the world—which, for the captain of the football team at Hampstead High, was nearly the truth. "Hey, Beth, you're pretty good friends with Adam Brainard, right?"

Beth couldn't believe it. Here she was, with the captain of the football team all to herself, and he was asking her about Adam.

"Yeah, sure," she answered, trying to sound offhand. "Why?"

"He was okay at practice yesterday," said Mike. "I mean, not great or anything—he doesn't have much experience—but, you know, pretty good."

"That's nice," said Beth, wishing Mike would get off the subject.

"Do you think—I mean, not that it's a big deal or

anything—but do you think he's serious about football? Because he might...well, I mean he never went out for football before. I was just wondering."

Beth was really surprised by Mike's questions. It dawned on her that Adam must have been so good at practice that Mike was actually concerned about the competition. *What a switch,* she thought, *the captain of the football team asking me for information about Adam!*

"Well, I don't know what Adam thinks now. I mean, he's changed so much since last year. He's always liked football—we used to go to a lot of games together, I mean, not together, but...well, you know what I mean. But I don't know whether he's really serious about it or not. I don't know *what* he's serious about anymore. What are you worried about?" she continued, teasing now. "That he's going to replace you as quarterback?"

Mike snorted. "Don't be ridiculous," he said scornfully. "I told you he wasn't great. *I'm* the one who's great," he said, only half joking.

"I've always thought so," said Beth, remembering her determination to flirt with Mike. *After all,* she said to herself, *a girl can't give up on the captain of the football team just because her best friend has suddenly become a hunk.* Beth showed her sweetest smile. "I hear Weird Noise is going to be at the Coliseum on the thirtieth..."

Beth chattered away as she and Mike walked the rest of the way to school. *I hope everyone sees me walking to school with Mike Collins,* she thought. *Especially Adam....No! I am not going to think about him!*

"Hi, Beth! Hi, Mike!" cried Robin, catching up

to them at the door.

"Hi, Robin," said Beth. "See you, Mike!" she called out as Mike kept walking—she wanted Robin to know they had been together.

"See you, Beth," said Mike over his shoulder.

"Ooh, Beth," said Robin teasingly. "Walking to school with the captain of the football team—pretty cool!"

"It's just my sneakers that attracted him," joked Beth, pleased with herself. "Adam always said Mike likes athletic girls."

"Oh yeah?" said Cynthia, appearing suddenly behind Robin and Beth. She looked terrific today with her long strawberry-blond hair streaming over her shoulders. "And what does Adam like? You should know, Beth, you two have been friends forever. C'mon, tell me—I really want to know."

Beth gritted her teeth, then tried to turn the grimace into a smile. "Gosh, Cynthia. He's changed so much over the summer, I really don't know. I mean, when he wrote to me from that wilderness camp, he was telling me how much he loved digging up long, slimy worms to go fishing with." Beth laughed silently at Cynthia's disgusted expression. "Maybe you could invite him over to look at the night crawlers in your backyard."

"How totally gross! We'll just have to reintroduce him to civilization...maybe at the Halloween Dance next month. You know I'm the head of the planning committee, don't you?"

Well, big deal for you, thought Beth. Fortunately, Robin broke in before she could say anything.

"C'mon, Beth, we've got to hurry. You know how Griffith is if you're even three seconds late. I hear she practically court-martials you."

Beth and Robin took off down the hallway. As they reached the door to the classroom, out of breath, smoothing loose hair back in place, there was Adam, smiling calmly at them.

"Hi, Beth. Hi, Robin. Finish your poetry assignment yet?"

Beth caught her breath. "Oh no, I thought it wasn't due until tomorrow!"

"Just checking." Beth and Adam had always teased each other like this, but now he seemed to be smiling at her in a completely new way. Not like "just a friend," but more like...

"Okay, class," drummed out Mrs. Griffith, "your attention, please," and Beth's thoughts had to be put on hold.

At lunchtime, Beth sat with Kate and the other cheerleaders, but she wasn't tuned into the conversation at all. She longed to confide in one of her friends, but she couldn't bring herself to. She felt like the character in the story "The Boy Who Cried Wolf"—she had said she was "madly in love" so many times that none of her friends would take her seriously if she talked to them about her strange new feelings for Adam. Still keeping her secret, she smiled and laughed at the right moments, but her inner thoughts remained her own.

Beth sleepwalked through the rest of her classes that afternoon, until her next-to-last period, drama class. *Adam*, she thought, waking up at last. *Adam will be there*. She walked in and there he was, waving at her and gesturing to an empty seat he had saved next to him.

"Oh, thanks, Adam," said Cynthia, appearing, seemingly, from nowhere. "You don't mind if I sit here," she said as she perched next to him.

"Uh, okay, I guess..." Adam answered as he looked at Beth and shrugged his shoulders.

How does she always turn up like that? wondered Beth. She certainly wasn't going to make a big deal about Cynthia grabbing the seat. *I can't let on how I feel about him*, thought Beth. *Least of all to Cynthia—that'll just make her want him more.*

"Now, what I'd like to do is break you up into groups of twos and threes, and have you memorize some short scenes to present at our next class." Mr. Willers, the drama coach, was the youngest teacher in the school, and all the kids liked him. Beth had had a tremendous crush on him last year. "This early in the term I really don't know all of your work, so I'm just going to assign you by pulling your names out of my hat." Mr. Willers sometimes wore an old-fashioned artist's beret, and he had it on his desk, filled with little scraps of paper. *What if I get matched up with Adam?* thought Beth. She looked around at the other girls in the class— including Cynthia. *And what if I don't?*

"Let's see, now," continued Mr. Willers. "I'll pick out two or three names at a time, and those will be the teams. Ready?" Beth held her breath as he read through half a dozen pairs of names. "Beth Patterson...Adam Brainard." Beth let the air out of her lungs in a burst, turning to smile at Adam—and Cynthia, who was, of course, sitting right next to him. She was smiling too, but it wasn't a very happy smile.

"…so if all you teams will get together and rehearse over the weekend, we can present our scenes in class next Monday." Mr. Willers looked around the class. "Okay?"

Then the bell rang to signal the end of the period.

Beth waited for Adam outside the classroom door. Her heart was pounding. *Was this a sign? Was fate throwing them together?* Beth smiled at the dramatic thoughts in her mind. *It's just another homework assignment,* she tried to tell herself. *Like studying math or chemistry or Spanish together.* But she knew it wasn't true. Mr. Willers had given them a romantic scene to do together, and Beth was very, very excited.

Cynthia came out of the classroom before Adam did. "Can you believe it?" she said. "You're doing a love scene with Mr. Gorgeous, and I'm playing an old maid in a scene with Mandy Harris! Some people have all the luck."

"Oh, come on, Cynthia. Just think—you'll have to do some real acting to play an old maid…" Beth stopped herself before she finished her sentence, but Cynthia had caught on to her train of thought and finished it for her.

"…but *you* won't have to act at all to look like you're in love with Adam Brainard, right?"

"Give me a break, will you, Cynthia?" said Beth, trying not to blush. "You know Adam's just a friend."

Beth looked over her shoulder, wondering what Cynthia was smiling about, and there was Adam. He had come out of the classroom while Beth and

Cynthia were talking. Beth was certain Adam had heard her last words. She would have given anything to take them back.

Trying not to let her feelings show, she said, "So, uh, Adam, when can you get together to rehearse?"

Adam replied, "Well, we've got extra football practice on Saturday morning—"

"Great, we've got cheerleading practice," Beth interrupted. "Why don't we meet outside the gym and then go to my house?"

"Terrific," said Adam. "I'll see you then."

"Well, now that you two friends have straightened that out," said Cynthia, emphasizing the word "friends," "how'd you like to walk me to my next class?" she asked Adam.

"Well, I—" began Adam.

"Great. Let's go," she said, taking Adam by the arm and briskly escorting him down the corridor and around the corner of the school building.

Beth stood alone in the hall, looking after them. *If I don't let him know how I feel pretty soon, Cynthia—or some other girl—is going to steal him right out from under my nose. But he's heard about all my crushes too. How will I ever make him take me seriously?*

Beth had always dreamed about falling in love. Why, then, did she feel so confused and miserable?

Chapter Three

Beth's radio alarm went off right at 7:00 A.M., and the song playing was Weird Noise's biggest hit. *Oh, they're so great,* she thought, still half dreaming. *Well, time to get ready for school....* She jerked herself into a sitting position, suddenly wide-awake. This was not another school day, this was Saturday! Saturday—first she had cheerleading practice and then a date to rehearse her scene for drama class with Adam! *This could be my big day,* she thought. *I'd better get it together.*

Beth practically jumped out of her bed, grabbing her robe as she headed for the bathroom to take a shower. *I've got to look absolutely great, even for cheerleading practice,* she thought. *Adam's going to be right across the field, and he'll see me. Oh, please don't let me make any stupid mistakes!*

Beth examined her collection of shampoos and conditioners, finally choosing the lemon-scented ones—bright, fresh, clean—*Just right for today,* she decided. She showered, put on a lemon-scented afterbath splash, and dried her hair. Then she ran back to her room to change into her practice uniform. *No jewelry,* she thought to herself. *No, wait—maybe only these tiny sapphire posts. They'll add just the right touch.*

Beth checked herself out in the mirror: the red shorts and red and white top looked great on her, she decided. She tossed her head, and her short dark hair fell into place around her face. Sometimes she wished she had long hair, like Cynthia's, so she could dress it up in different ways—ponytails, curled into ringlets, or tied back with a ribbon—but her short cut was so easy to take care of, and it was cooler in the summer, and for practice. *Not too much makeup*—it would just run in the heat and make her look stupid.... *Well, maybe just a little raspberry lip gloss and some blusher and mascara.* She packed some jeans and a T-shirt to put on after practice, and was ready to go.

Beth ate a light breakfast and started jogging to the fields to warm up before the 9:00 A.M. practice —she really wanted to be in top shape today.

"Hi, Beth. You look great." Jogging along beside her was...Adam.

"Oh, hi, Adam," said Beth, trying to sound casual. Her heart was suddenly beating much faster than it needed to for the pace she was running at. "How's football going?"

"Terrific! Coach says I'm a natural. I might even make the starting team—and this is my first time playing organized football!" Adam blushed. "I guess I sound like a little kid, but this is all really exciting for me. I've never really been a jock before."

"I guess they really worked you out at that wilderness camp," said Beth. "But please don't overdo it today—I want you full of energy for our rehearsal this afternoon."

28

"No need to worry about that," said Adam, looking at Beth with his frank blue eyes. "I always have lots of energy when I'm with you."

Beth nearly gasped. Could it be? Did Adam feel the same way she did?

During practice, it took all of Beth's self-control to concentrate on the exercise and routines—she kept wanting to look over at the football team, especially since she could hear the coach calling out things like, "Good work, Brainard!" She even thought she heard Adam's voice calling out some plays—could the coach be grooming him for quarterback? She couldn't believe it. Mike Collins had been quarterback for a long time. No wonder he'd been worried about Adam the other day.

Cynthia bumped into Beth during one tumbling routine, spilling them both onto the grass. Beth got a scratch down one side of her leg from some twigs on the field. *Great,* she thought, *just what I need today—a few yucky bruises and bumps for my love scene with Adam.*

While she was getting back onto her feet, Beth glanced over at the football practice—and saw Adam looking right at her.

"Hey, Brainard, keep your eyes on *this* field, buddy."

"Sorry, Coach," Beth heard Adam shout back. *I think he actually cares about me!* she thought.

Beth dropped her head so no one could see the smile on her face, and got back into line for the next routine. Then she lifted her head high and concentrated on what she had to do.

When cheerleading was finished, she ran over to football practice to see Adam. When he saw her, he came over.

"Are you okay, Beth? I saw that fall." Adam was looking at her, his eyes full of concern.

"It was nothing, really," said Beth. "I just scratched my leg—I'll clean it up in the locker room. How about you, Adam—did I really hear you calling some plays?"

"Yeah," said Adam, looking down at his sneakers. "Coach says I ought to learn everything about the game, and quarterback is where you learn how all the pieces fit together."

"That's great," Beth said with a grin. "I have to change and get my stuff. I'll meet you out here in fifteen minutes."

"I'll be here," said Adam, looking after her as she ran to the girls' locker room.

Beth showered and changed in record time, and hurried back out to the field. Cynthia had come over to Adam. They were sitting down, and Cynthia was leaning back on her hands, her long strawberry-blond hair streaming down her back, shining in the sun.

"Ready, Adam?" Beth said, smiling in a friendly way, trying to look as though she wasn't the least bit jealous of Cynthia.

"Now, don't you two get carried away with this scene," teased Cynthia. "I'll see you tonight, Adam."

"Bye, Cynthia," Adam said as he and Beth walked off together.

"Tonight?" Beth asked Adam, sounding as nonchalant as she could. "What are you and Cynthia doing tonight?"

"Oh, we're going to see that new movie playing in town," said Adam. "It's supposed to be really funny."

What about me? Beth cried out in her thoughts. *I'm the one you should take to the movies. I'm the one you should care about....*

"Well, I hope you have a good time," she said, making a face even as she spoke the words. *What a dumb thing to say,* she thought.

"You know, Cynthia's really been paying a lot of attention to me lately. Do you think maybe she might like me?" asked Adam.

Beth felt her heart sink—this was the last thing in the world she wanted to happen. Adam asking her about other girls? She just wanted him to be interested in *her!* Beth managed to croak out some compliments about Cynthia...fun to be with, good sense of humor. She didn't want Adam to think she would put down other girls just because he was interested in them.

Besides, I haven't even told Adam how I feel about him, thought Beth. *Cynthia's being much more honest than I am, in some ways. Maybe if I tell him today.... Oh, it'll never work! He just won't believe me.* Beth was utterly miserable. How on earth was she ever going to be able to concentrate on their romantic scene together?

Adam was talking, and she hadn't even been paying attention. "A lot of girls seem to be reacting differently toward me this year," he was saying. "I don't know whether it's because I'm taller, or because I'm going out for football, or what. I really don't know who I can trust—except for you, Beth. I know you better than anyone. You don't feel any differently about me, do you?" Adam looked her right in the eyes.

Yes, yes, I do, Beth wanted to shout. But she held it in, and quickly dropped her eyes to avoid his glance. "No, of course not, Adam. You're my friend, same as always." Beth was close to tears. *But I want you to be more, now!*

Adam was going on: "Great. So you'll be able to help me like always. Only now, you can tell me which girls are really sincere, and which ones are just after me for my new packaging."

Beth didn't answer, but Adam didn't seem to notice.

"Well, here we are," he said. "I'm starved. How about getting something to eat before we get started."

Great. Now we're talking about food, thought Beth as they headed for the kitchen. *Very romantic. Maybe this is all crazy. Maybe I should forget Adam and concentrate on some other guy, like Mike Collins.*

"How's Mike doing this season?" Beth asked Adam, continuing her train of thought out loud.

Adam was making one of his usual sandwiches with about five different types of meat stacked one on top of the other. He was about to add the mayonnaise and lettuce, completing his masterpiece. "Oh, you know, 'I'm the greatest,' stuff like that. He's pretty conceited. But he sure is a good player," said Adam. "How come you want to know?"

"Oh, we were walking to school together the other day, talking and stuff," said Beth, "and I had a feeling he was kind of worried about how he was doing—or the competition this year." She watched

Adam carefully. What part of what she said would he react to?

"You were walking to school with Mike?" asked Adam, the hand holding his sandwich pausing before it got to his mouth. "I didn't know you two were friends."

Bingo! thought Beth. *You didn't care about his being worried about football—you cared that he was walking with me!*

"Yeah, I think he's really cute, and you know me," said Beth, wondering how far she could go with this.

"Let's get to work on that scene," said Adam, changing the subject abruptly, "or we won't have enough time to rehearse before I have to go meet Cynthia."

That stopped Beth in her tracks. "You're right," she said somewhat sternly. "Let's get to work."

Beth and Adam went into the living room and started reading the scene aloud. It was a very dramatic scene—a girl suspecting her boyfriend of seeing another girl, and the boyfriend accusing her of seeing another boy. *Perfect,* thought Beth. *I'll hardly have to work at all to make this totally realistic.*

Beth had already memorized her part completely, and was a little annoyed that Adam kept having to look at the book. "You're not going to read from the book in class, are you?" she asked him, implying from her tone of voice that his answer had better be no.

"No. Cynthia said I could go over to her house after the movie tonight and she'd run lines with me."

Beth remembered Mr. Willers's instructions: "When you have a strong emotion, use it in your work." She didn't say anything about Adam's rehearsing with Cynthia, she just started one of her speeches from the scene.

"How dare you tell me you've been faithful to me! I know better. I know where you've been, and I know who you've been seeing—and I know what you've been doing with her. So don't try to act innocent with me! Look me in the eyes and tell me it's not true. I've known you for far too long, Brian. I can tell when you're lying, and you're lying right now."

Beth's delivery was so dramatic that Adam didn't say a word. He just stared at her with his mouth open, eyes unblinking, as if waiting for her to continue.

"Well?" said Beth, a little angrily. "Can't you even *read* your lines? We're on page fifty-four."

"Hey," said Adam, "I'm impressed. You know, you really can act."

"Flattery will get you nowhere," said Beth, wanting to avoid any personal discussion. "Let's just do the scene." She was having trouble expressing hurt, angry feelings in real life, so she needed an outlet—and acting was giving her that outlet.

*

Beth and Adam continued to work on the scene until five-thirty, when Adam said, a little reluctantly, "I have to go now."

"Oh sure," said Beth stiffly. "You'd better not be

late. I hope you'll do a lot more work on your lines with Cynthia."

"Beth...hey, Beth, the scene's over, okay?" said Adam softly. "It's Beth and Adam here, not Sylvia and Brian. Lighten up, okay?"

"Sorry, Adam. I guess I got a little carried away." Beth was somewhat embarrassed by her outburst. "Just memorize those lines, okay?"

"Sure," said Adam, packing up his books and notes. Then his expression changed, and he turned to look directly at Beth. His voice sounded different as he began to talk. "Listen, I don't know how to tell you this, but—"

"Yes?" asked Beth, too quickly. Adam's face closed up again, and he looked away.

"Oh, it's nothing, I guess," he said, almost mumbling. "I don't know. Everything's just...strange, that's all."

"What's strange?" said Beth, wanting to draw him out, get him to stay and talk to her. "Tell me."

Adam looked at her again. "I just feel like we're all changing, like I'm not sure who anybody is anymore. Or maybe I'm just the one that's changing, so everybody seems different to me because *I'm* different. Or maybe—oh, forget it." He shook his head.

No, no, Adam, thought Beth. *I know what you mean. I just don't know how to tell you...that I think I love you!*

"I won't forget it," Beth said out loud. "Have fun at the movie." Somehow, Adam's last outburst wiped out Beth's jealousy over his date with Cynthia—she knew he would never be able to talk to *her*

35

like that.

"Thanks," said Adam. "And thanks for the rehearsal."

They walked to the front door together, and Adam turned to kiss her quickly on the cheek. "I guess I'll see you Monday," he said.

Beth was stunned. "See you Monday," she replied. He went out the door, and started walking down the path. Beth watched his back, his long legs striding gracefully across the flagstones. He was turning around.

"Bye!" he called out, waving.

Beth waved back, not trusting her voice. *He kissed me!* was all she could think. He had never done that before, no friendly pecks on the cheek, no silly gestures like "kissing a lady's hand," nothing. Adam had never been that type of guy. *Maybe it's just happening to us, all of us, like Adam said. Maybe we're all changing.* Beth shook her head, trying to clear her thoughts. *Everything is strange. Adam was right.*

Beth felt a lump in her throat, and wondered why she was about to cry. She wasn't even eighteen years old yet, and she was feeling her life speeding by like a freight train. She was traveling into strange territory. And unsure ground was approaching much too fast. "But I'm not ready to grow up yet," whispered Beth. "I'm just not ready. I wonder if anyone is."

Beth turned, walked upstairs to her bedroom, and took down Bunky, the big stuffed panda bear that she hadn't played with since she was twelve years old. It was way up on top of her shelves, and she had to stand on her desk chair to reach it. She sat cross-legged on her bed, hugged her bear, and cried bittersweet tears into its soft, black and white fake fur. "Who am I, Bunky?" Beth sobbed.

Chapter Four

Dear Diary:

You won't believe this. Mr. Willers loved the scene! He said the work was perfect. Our class was really quiet after it was finished, so I know everyone thought it was just great.

Adam knew all his lines, too. I guess he and Cynthia worked on them for a long time that night. Boy, I didn't have any problem being jealous—she kissed him right before the scene began and wished him luck! "Break a leg," she said. "Think of all our work together Saturday night." Can you believe it, Diary? I don't understand how she can be so obvious.

But that's not the worst part of it. I've been trying not to write this, but I guess I have to. Adam had to do the scene with *Cynthia*. Not by choice, of course, but he had to do it anyway. I woke up this morning with a giant case of laryngitis. Just like in the movies. Cynthia knew my lines from rehearsing with Adam. She was *delighted* to be able to help me out by filling in. And I had to sit in class and watch! That really hurt.

Adam didn't seem to have any big objections either. Of course, why should he? I mean, Cynthia's cute and funny, so why should he complain about doing a scene with her? Why should he do anything with me instead of her? Just because he can talk to me? Do guys care about that kind of stuff?

Who am I kidding? (How many people are writing in this diary, anyway?) I know Adam does care, even though he hasn't talked to me again about those serious growing-up-type thoughts he sort of mentioned the other day. I'm a little frightened to talk about them myself—do you know, I took down Bunky the Panda after all these years, and told him about the many changes I've been through since I used to play with him all the time? Just to let him know what's happening to me. I've been friends with Adam just as long as I've had Bunky, and I'd really like to sit and talk with *him* about all my new feelings—he could talk back, not like a stuffed animal! Sometimes I wish you could talk back too, Diary—you know me better than anyone. These days I'm not sure I know myself.

* * *

Dear Diary:
Cheerleading is really great this fall. The team is totally together, and I love our new routine! When I'm tumbling in time to the music, I feel like everything's right with the world. I just forget all my problems and flip, turn, kick, jump— well, you get the idea.

Practice is really great for guy-watching too. The football team always works out at the same time we do, and I can see Adam…and the other guys…really working out. Adam's still doing well—Mike Collins keeps talking to me about him. Or do you think that's just an excuse for Mike to talk to me, Diary? Is it possible? Could Mike Collins, captain of the Hampstead High Vikings, really be interested in me? (Do I care?) (Of course you care; don't be silly. You'd be weird not to care.) (But I'm in love with Adam.) QUIET!!! Too many writers spoil the journal. Now, where was I? Oh, yes. Football. Cheerleading. Mike and Adam. Adam and Mike.

I feel like I'm trapped between old and new, Diary. Do I go with the old "crush" me, or the new "true love" me? I'm all mixed up. If Adam and Mike both asked me to the Halloween Dance, who would I go with? (If only I should have such a dilemma!) No, really—who would I go with? The sad truth is, Diary…I really don't know.

* * *

Dear Diary:

Cynthia's been going on and on about the Halloween Dance, that it's going to be "the most awesome event of the fall season," and all sorts of junk like that. It's all because she's the committee head, and thinks she's so important.

I hope Adam's going to ask me to go to the dance with him. There's a small snag in my plans. Mr. Willers teamed Adam and Cynthia to do another scene together, and it was as good as the first one. I hope that won't get to be a big problem for me. Adam and I see each other in drama and English classes, and across the field at cheerleading and football practice nearly every day. Who else would he ask anyway? Cynthia? I think she's got her eyes on some of the senior guys.... Who am I kidding, Diary? She throws herself at Adam whenever she gets the chance. Oh no, what if *she* asks *him!* He'd never turn her down.

What should I do, Diary? Should I ask him first? Or maybe he won't understand. (How could he not understand it, dummy—you're in love with him.) But maybe he'll...he'll...say no! What if he still thinks of me as just a friend? Should I tell him how I really feel? Or will that just scare him off? And how *do* I really feel anyway?

* * *

Dear Diary:

Gross! Double-gross! Today we finally dissected a cat in biology! YUCK! I refuse to write any more about this. It was too disgusting to think about for one second more than absolutely necessary.

Kate and Robin and I went out after cheerleading practice today. I'm dying to tell one of them how I feel about Adam, but I just don't know how to do it. After years of talking to them about all those crushes of mine, I'm worried they just wouldn't take me seriously. So I just kind of go blah-blah-blah about Mike Collins, or some rock star or another, and pretend I'm the same old Beth. None of them seems to notice anything different about me...although they do keep talking about Adam, how different he looks, how all the girls (especially Cynthia!) think he's really gorgeous, etc., etc. I drink a lot of diet sodas or go to the bathroom when they start *those* conversations.

No, I still haven't decided what to do about the Halloween Dance and Adam and Cynthia and all that stuff. I'm going to put it off for a while yet... the dance is still a few weeks away, after all. I wonder what I should wear...

* * *

Dear Diary:

I had lunch with Mike Collins today!!! Can you believe it?! He actually left the jock table to come and sit with me. (Yes, he's still pumping me for information about Adam, but I think all these conversations we've been having are beginning to have an effect on him....In other words, I think he's starting to like me!) But you know, Diary... I'm so nervous around him. Captain of the football team, great catch and all that...but it's not the same as what I feel when I'm with Adam. With Adam, I feel excited, like my heart pounds and my blood rushes...but I feel *comfortable* too. It's hard to explain.

I'll tell you, though: *everyone* stared at Mike and me eating lunch together. Robin grabbed my arm on the way out of the cafeteria and said, "Way to go, Beth!" No one ever does that when they see me and Adam together—probably because everyone knows we're "only friends."

Adam's getting really popular, too, this year. I see kids from our drama class stopping him in the hall and saying how good his scene was, or guys in the cafeteria coming up to talk to him about football and stuff. I wonder how he feels about all this—I mean, Adam always had lots of friends, but he was never one of those "superstar" kids, you know, one of the kids that *everybody* knows. I guess that's what he was talking about at our first rehearsal—that he knows he can trust me, because I've *always* liked him. He doesn't know whether his new "friends" are really friends, or just impressed with his recent superstar status.

And what about me? Am I falling in love with him because of who he really is, or because of all the changes he's been through? You'd better look at yourself, Beth. Maybe you're just as superficial and hypocritical as all the other kids. I mean, why didn't you fall in love with Adam last year? Wasn't he just as nice and friendly then? Or are you only attracted by his looks?

But…but…I'm changing, too. That's why this is all so confusing. Yes, Adam's different than he was last year…but so am I (sort of). And I know the way I feel is the real thing, I just know it! (Then why are you so excited about having lunch with Mike Collins, huh?) (Well, yeah, but I'm also worried about Cynthia getting too close to Adam.) (Sure, but why? Because you really love Adam…or because you don't want to lose

such a great catch to another girl?) QUIET!!!
Enough writing for tonight. I've got a lot to think
about before I fall asleep, and it's already late.

* * *

Dear Diary:
    HOORAY! An A!! An A from Mrs. Griffith!!!
Isn't that incredible? I must say, I did deserve it: I
worked harder on that paper than on anything
I've ever done in my life. I held it up in class for
Adam to see the big red A marked on the cover,
and he gave me the biggest smile and a thumbs-
up sign!
    PLUS...I'm the front tumbler in our third
cheerleading routine! I'm so excited. I really have
to be PERFECT: Everyone on the squad is supposed to follow my lead in terms of timing, and
style, and everything. If anything goes wrong, it
will be MY FAULT.
    Adam congratulated me when I saw him after
practice today. But WHY hasn't he asked me to
that dumb Halloween Dance yet? The suspense
is killing me. Oh, Diary...you don't suppose he's
seen how much attention Mike Collins has been
giving me lately, and *he's* jealous? I think that
he's still being my "friend"—I always told him
how much I adored Mike Collins, and now he's
giving me plenty of room to "go for it"! How can
I tell him it's *him* I really want?
    I've just got to pull myself together and tell him
soon. We're meeting to discuss an English project
on Saturday after practice, and I'll tell him then,

absolutely. And he'll ask me to the dance, and then he'll kiss me, and everything will be just perfect.

* * *

Dear Diary:

Guess what? MIKE COLLINS ASKED ME TO GO TO THE MOVIES WITH HIM SATURDAY NIGHT!!! I nearly dropped my notebooks, I was so nervous. (I mean, I could hardly say, No, sorry, I have an English project meeting with Adam Brainard Saturday afternoon and I'm planning to tell him I love him, so I really can't go with you to the movies Saturday night.) (Or could I?) (No, you couldn't.) I'm too excited to write any more today! Good night.

* * *

Dear Diary:

Practice was fine; my meeting with Adam went great, as usual (although he did seem a little distant...maybe he knew I was going to the movies with Mike afterwards), and after the movies, Mike and I went out for hamburgers, and HE ASKED ME TO THE HALLOWEEN DANCE!!! (Surprise, Diary—betcha thought I'd write that first thing, huh?) Well, I acted very coy, said I'd have to think about it and thank-you-so-much-for-asking and I'd tell him on Monday. Kate would have been proud of me! I've never played hard to get so coolly in my life!

Well, Diary, it's happened: I'm going to have

to choose between Mike and Adam to go to the dance with. Of course, Adam still hasn't asked me, but I'm sure he will. In fact, I'll call him tomorrow and tell him about Mike asking me, and I'm sure he'll say, "Go with me, instead." And when I say yes, and he realizes I turned down Mike Collins, captain of the football team and object of my crushes for the past umpteen years, he'll finally know how much I love him!

Monday morning, Beth headed off to school with high hopes. The sun was shining, Beth was dressed in her best fall clothes, and she felt just terrific. She hadn't been able to reach Adam by phone the day before, but that was okay; it would be better to tell him in person anyway. She couldn't wait to see his face when she said yes, after he asked her to the Halloween Dance.

Beth got to her locker, and was hanging up her jacket and getting out her books for first class, when she heard Adam's voice around the corner. She hurriedly grabbed her notebooks and bag, and ran off in the direction his voice was coming from, saying in her mind, "I tried to call you yesterday, but it's better to see you in person and…"

Adam was talking to Cynthia, and Beth could overhear the conversation as she approached the corner. She stayed out of sight, and heard Cynthia saying, "Great, Adam, we'll get here early so I can oversee the set-up committee. Can you pick me up at my house around five-thirty?"

Adam smiled, but he was fidgeting a little. "You know, Cynthia, I wanted to talk to Beth about—"

"About what?" asked Cynthia. "The dance?

Mike Collins asked her to the dance on Saturday, after their date for the movies. She called Kate, and Kate called Robin, and Robin called me. Everyone knows about it. She'd never turn him down. Not even for you," she concluded. "You mean, she didn't call you and tell you all about it? I thought you two were old friends."

Beth stood absolutely frozen, biting her lip, fighting back tears. Why, oh why, did she call Kate and tell her? She'd sworn her to secrecy, but she knew that she really wanted Kate to call everyone and tell them. *But only because then Adam would know how much I love him when I turned Mike down!* Beth thought.

What could she do now? *Nothing*, she decided, and backed slowly and quietly down the hall, hoping Adam and Cynthia didn't know she had overheard their conversation. Now she had to accept Mike's invitation and forget about going to the dance with Adam. Cynthia had gotten there first, and Beth had no one to blame but herself.

"Hey, Beth, how you doing?" It was Mike Collins, waking her out of her daze. "So, what's the good word?" he asked, grinning, totally sure of himself. No girl had ever turned down an invitation of his before—why should she?

"Oh, hi, Mike, I'm fine," said Beth without much conviction. How come she'd never noticed he was such a show-off and so self-centered? "I guess the good word is yes."

"Well, sound a little cheerful about it, please! Pick you up around seven?" Mike said.

"That'd be fine," said Beth. "Gotta go to class, or I'll be late. See ya."

*

Dear Diary:

The worst has happened again. Adam and Cynthia are going to the Halloween Dance together. I let it go too long.

Oh, yeah, Mike Collins is my date. I know I should be excited, but I'm not. Don't ask. I'm going through too many changes, Diary, and most of them hurt a lot.

Too depressed to write any more. Good night.

Chapter Five

Posters lined the hallways at school: Come to the Halloween Dance, Dance Under the October Moon, Costume Ball! The posters were colorful and inviting, promising an exciting time for everyone. Cynthia had set up a committee to cover every aspect of the dance: publicity and promotion, entertainment, refreshments, box office, and a cleanup crew to break it all down when the dance was over.

Cynthia could hardly contain herself. She was like the queen bee overseeing all the different committees. She was practically humming as she buzzed up and down the hallways at school, stopping to talk to all the different kids under her "command." But, no matter how busy she was, whenever Adam walked by, she could stop whatever she was doing to talk with him. She knew she had Hampstead High's latest catch as her date, and she didn't want anyone to forget it—least of all Adam Brainard.

Beth walked through the halls at school, forcing herself to hold her head up high. After all, she was going to the dance with the captain of the football team; that was a super big deal, wasn't it? All the other girls certainly seemed to think so; they all stopped her to whisper congratulations, mixed with giggles of excitement. If it wasn't for all the attention she was getting, Beth would have walked around with her head down and her heart sunk somewhere near her feet. That's how she felt inside, but she had to keep it a secret.

English and drama classes were difficult because she was forced to see Adam—and because of the subject matter. English usually consisted of discussions of lost hopes or lost loves in the poetry they were studying. Drama was the hardest: they were doing *Romeo and Juliet*. Beth chewed her lips, ground her teeth, bit her fingernails, gnawed on pencils—anything to keep her mind off all the sadness in the play...and in her own life.

Usually Kate would have picked up on Beth's misery, but she seemed distracted about something this term. She didn't talk much about boys, mostly just school stuff—although she did congratulate Beth on going to the dance with Mike Collins.

It was Robin who found out the truth on Wednesday. She walked into the girls' bathroom and saw Beth, her head buried in her chest, her arms wrapped around her shoulders, looking as if she were about to cry.

"Beth!" cried Robin. "What's the matter?"

"Oh, Robin," said Beth, "if I tell you, you'll never believe me."

"Probably not," said Robin. "I can't imagine why anyone who's going to the Halloween Dance with the greatest catch at Hamster High would possibly look as if she's about to cry." Robin was talking in a light, joking tone, hoping to cheer Beth up, but she could see it wasn't working. "But try me, Beth. You never know. Maybe I could help," she concluded more seriously.

"Robin... Robin, I don't want to go to the dance with Mike. I want to go with...with..."

"With whom?" Robin always remembered to say "whom" since Mrs. Griffith had given her a B on one of her papers where she'd forgotten to.

"With...Adam Brainard!" There! She had finally said it to someone.

"Adam! How could it be Adam?" said Robin, almost in disbelief. "You've never let on that you're interested in him at all. Whenever we start talking about him, you just clam up or leave the room, or say he's just a friend, or—I guess it *does* make sense...Adam..."

"I know, I know," said Beth miserably. "I didn't want anyone to know. I was afraid you'd all laugh at me, or say it's just another one of my crushes. But I feel differently about Adam; I really do. I don't know if it's because he's changed so much, or because I've changed, but I really...really..."

"...really love him?" Robin finished the sentence for her. Beth nodded her head, unable to speak. "Oh, Beth, why did you keep it to yourself? You shouldn't have worried about what we'd say. Why didn't you tell one of us? Listen, I'll tell Adam, and I'm sure he'd rather go to the dance with you than with Cynthia—"

"Don't you dare!" shouted Beth, really alarmed. "I don't want him to find out like that, through the grapevine. He'll think I just have a silly crush on him, like all the other girls do, because he's so good-looking this year. This is *serious!*"

"Okay, okay, Beth, calm down, it's all right. I won't say anything to him, I promise." Robin looked at Beth inquisitively. "This is the real thing, isn't it?"

Again Beth nodded, not trusting her voice. "You're the first person I've told, Robin. You've got to promise me you won't tell anyone—*anyone*, not even Kate, or any of the other girls, and certainly not Adam. Promise!"

"I promise, Beth; I promise. Don't worry. I won't tell a soul," said Robin, crossing her heart. "But what are you going to do?"

"I don't know," said Beth, trying to pull herself back together. "I guess I'll just go to the dance with Mike Collins, and try to steal a few moments with Adam while I'm there. One thing's for sure: Cynthia's going to have a lot to do as the head of the dance committee."

"Wait a minute," said Robin. "Haven't you told Adam anything yet? I mean, does he have *any* idea how you feel? You two see each other every day, between English and drama class and practice and all that."

"No," said Beth, "he doesn't know. I haven't even given him the tiniest hint. He still thinks I think of him as just a friend. I'm going to tell him, Robin, really I will—I just don't know when...or how."

"Well," said Robin, "you've let me in on the biggest secret I've heard all term. If I can help at all, just ask me. And please keep me up to date! If I can't talk to anyone else about this, you'd better keep me posted, or I'll burst!"

"Okay, okay," said Beth. "I will; I promise." She took a deep breath, then turned to the sink and rinsed her face with cold water. "We'd better get going or we'll be late for class."

*

Friday, the day of the dance, had finally arrived. All the kids were talking about it. The entertainment committee had gotten one of the hottest local bands to play; Cynthia had actually managed to get a local deejay to work between sets; and Mr. Willers, the drama teacher, was going to be the MC. Everyone had worked on his or her costume for weeks—some of the girls were dressing as hot rock stars or music video look-alikes, and a few boys were coming as movie monsters and comic-book heroes. Several creative types were going to wear weird outfits like "a tube of toothpaste" or "a computer." *But how are they going to dance?* wondered Beth.

Mike had wanted to go as a football player and a cheerleader. "Oh no," said Beth. "That's *real* life. This is a chance for us to be creative and different." She had finally convinced him they should go as space explorers.

Her mom helped her make their costumes out of shiny silver fabric: a flashy tunic and intricately designed pants for Mike, who carried a really unusual jewel-encrusted sword they found at a local costume store; and a teeny-tiny shiny miniskirt and top for Beth, who completed her outfit with sparkly pantyhose and silver go-go boots she had snapped up at a nearby thrift shop. Mike was going to wear outer-space wraparound sunglasses, and Beth was going to decorate her face with stage makeup—she would look bizarre but beautiful. She knew she would look great. *But how will I feel inside?* she thought.

What is Adam going to wear? wondered Beth.

She had asked him the other day what he and Cynthia were going to wear, but he wouldn't tell. "It's a surprise," he said as he smiled mischievously at her. "Even Cynthia doesn't know what I'm going to wear."

Beth shook her head to clear the image of Adam from her mind. *Enough of that,* she thought, *just concentrate on getting ready for Mike. He's going to be here any minute.*

Mike had borrowed his dad's car, and picked up Beth at seven-thirty. She had already put the finishing touches on her makeup, and Mike smiled when he saw her: she had green and silver swirls curling up the sides of her face, making her cheekbones stand out beautifully. Her eyes were framed in large feathery touches of gold and peacock blue, giving her a wide-eyed, surprised look. Her hair was topped with a silver cap with gold and green silk tassels. Beth truly looked like a royal creature from another planet, a space explorer from another time.

Mike looked great in his silver spaceman's outfit. It had a green sash cutting a bold diagonal across his chest, emphasizing his broad shoulders. With his narrow, wraparound sunglasses and his antique sword, he looked like a warrior from a space-adventure movie. He and Beth would make a beautiful couple at the dance—they might even win a prize for best costume.

"Hi, Beth," said Mike. "You look really great. That makeup is awesome."

"I told you it would be," said Beth. "Your sunglasses look really cool, too."

"Are you ready to go?" asked Mike.

"I feel like we should fire up the spaceship and hit the sky!" said Beth. She felt excited and happy— she wasn't going to let the fact that Adam and Cynthia were together ruin this night. She looked beautiful, her date was the captain of the football team—what more could she want? "To be with the one guy you really love," said a little voice inside her.

Fortunately, the day of the dance actually fell on Halloween, so Beth and Mike didn't feel weird going out in public in their costumes: The streets were filled with kids of all ages trick-or-treating in every imaginable outfit. The two got into Mike's father's car and headed off on the short ride to Hampstead High.

The entrance to the school was jammed with students in costume, waiting to get into the dance. The kids who were at the door wore scary rubber monster masks, and growled, "Go right in" as Beth and Mike gave them their tickets.

Robin was right inside the entrance, dressed as a fairy princess, wearing a short, heavenly gown of some diaphanous material and carrying a magic wand with a glittery star on the end. Her hair was gently caught up in a bun with tiny white flowers, and delicate wisps curled around her face. The minute she saw Mike and Beth enter the building, she ran up to them.

"You two look absolutely *fabulous*!" gushed Robin. "No other couple looks half as great," she added meaningfully to Beth.

"Thanks, Robin," said Beth, smiling happily. "You look beautiful."

"Yeah," said Mike, looking at Robin appreciatively, "that fabric is quite, uh, sheer, isn't it?" He hastily added, "It's a very pretty dress," not wanting her to feel he was coming on to her. "Did you make it yourself?"

"My mom helped me," admitted Robin, "but I designed it all by myself."

"Well, come on, you guys—let's go into the dance," said Beth. "I want to see what everything looks like."

The three of them entered the auditorium together, and looked appreciatively at the great job the decorating committee had done. Orange and green spotlights from old theater productions lit the room in an eerie glow, while stuffed witches, ghosts, and scarecrows hung from the ceiling fixtures, giving the room a gruesome aspect. Jack-o'-lanterns flickered around the edges of the room and on the refreshment tables. Orange and black crepe paper, and cardboard cutouts of ghosts and skeletons lined the walls.

The band was already onstage and warmed up. The room was full of kids in costumes and when the music started with a bang, the dance floor was suddenly filled with all sorts of creatures: princesses and dragons, monsters and rock stars, witches and ghosts, heroes and villains, and animals of every stripe.

"Look at Cynthia and Adam," Robin whispered to Beth. "Can you believe it?"

Beth could see Cynthia in a beautiful red silk gown and matching high, pointed hat with a veil, obviously a medieval princess. But where was Adam?

Then, as she watched, Beth broke up laughing: Cynthia was edging away from a guy at her side—and no wonder! He was dressed in filthy, slimy rags, with hundreds of wiggly plastic worms attached to his body, like some horrid swamp creature or partially eaten corpse risen from the grave—a truly disgusting costume. And who was this repulsive creature? Adam, of course.

Beth remembered his writing to her about digging up worms at wilderness camp, and how Cynthia had been totally grossed out by that, and she laughed some more. *Adam has really outdone himself*, she thought. *But it really took some guts for him to come in that costume. No one is going to want to dance with him looking like that.* Beth stopped laughing at Adam's horrible costume—and at Cynthia cringing beside him—and she began to smile. *This could be my chance to show Adam how I really feel about him*, she thought.

"Excuse me, Mike, Robin," said Beth, "I have to go and say hello to a special friend of mine."

Beth walked across the room, past Cynthia, and right up to Adam—whom everyone was avoiding, walking by and saying "gross," "disgusting," and so on.

"Hark!" Beth cried dramatically. "Let it be known that I, Princess of Worms, have come to claim my subject, Sir Adam Wormwood! Come with me and be my Prince."

"Ah, sweet Princess!" said Adam in a deep tone of voice, falling immediately in line with the story—the result of their improvisations in acting class.

"You have come to free me from the bondage of this terrible world where a man is judged only on appearances! At last I will assume my rightful role."

Beth and Adam walked together onto the dance floor with everyone watching them in amazement. They danced the first dance together, smiling at each other and laughing at the whole silly situation. Cynthia and Mike were both watching in wonder. Cynthia couldn't figure out why Adam had picked such a gross costume for their date, and how Beth could bear to be near him; Mike was embarrassed that his date was dancing the first dance with someone else—and worst of all that it was Adam, his competition on the football team, looking like something from *Revenge of the Swamp Monster*.

It seemed as though it might be a perfect evening for Beth and Adam. They danced the first couple of dances together, got something to eat, and shared a few jokes—all the time completely ignoring their dates. Then Adam said, "Wait here, Beth. I have a surprise for you." And he disappeared out of the auditorium.

Mike, too proud to act hurt, came up to Beth and said, "You know, Beth, it was real sweet of you to make your friend Adam feel comfortable even though he wore that disgusting costume. But now that you've done your charity work for the night, how about a dance with *me*?"

"Why, sure," said Beth, smiling sweetly at Mike. She was so happy about how things were going with Adam that she felt as though she were on top of the world. Beth and Mike swept onto the dance floor, their silvery costumes reflecting the orange and green lights of the auditorium. Robin was right—

there wasn't a better-looking couple at the dance.

Cynthia was watching them from the side of the room, wishing her date hadn't shown up dressed as king of the worms. Cool kids never wore totally gross or nerdy outfits—they left that for the weird, creative types, who didn't have anything to lose. Why was Adam doing this? He was really popular this year. He had no reason to act like such a geek. Cynthia busied herself conferring with a few of the other kids from the dance committee, and tried to pretend she wasn't insulted her date had disappeared—she was, in fact, relieved that Adam and his horrible outfit were gone.

Then, suddenly, he came back. He had washed off the layers of slime and dirt, removed the worms, and was dressed as an archeologist/adventurer complete with pith helmet, short khaki pants, pistol, desert boots, and bullwhip. He looked super-gorgeous, as though he'd just stepped off the movie screen. His hair was wet, and combed back across his head, and his smile added to it all.

Cynthia spotted him immediately and rushed over to him. "Oh, Adam," she cried, "at last you've come! If only you'd been here a few minutes ago, you could have rescued me from this dreadful swamp creature that was oozing worms all over me."

Robin had come up to join them. "Wow, Adam," she said, looking at him favorably. "How'd you change so fast?"

"Quick shower in the locker room—I had my knapsack in there with a change of clothes," said Adam casually. "Where's Beth?"

"Out on the dance floor with her outer-space hunk," said Cynthia, taking Adam by the arm.

"Now, why don't you and I follow their example?"

"Charmed, sweet princess," said Adam, sweeping off his pith helmet. He hesitated for a moment, then took one last glance at Beth and Mike dancing together, and went off with Cynthia.

"It was really sweet of Beth to dance with you when you were dressed in that horrible outfit," said Cynthia to Adam as they were dancing. "I guess you two must be really good friends."

"Yeah," said Adam, somewhat reluctantly, as he watched Beth and Mike laughing together as they danced. "I guess that's what we are."

Beth and Mike took a break from dancing to get some refreshments. Robin stopped them on their way to the table and pulled Beth off to one side.

"Did you see Adam's new outfit?" whispered Robin. "He looks just incredible! But Cynthia's got a pretty tight grasp on him now. You're going to have a hard time getting his attention again."

Beth turned and saw Cynthia and Adam dancing together, and her heart froze. *How could he?* she thought to herself. *After the way she treated him before....Oh no, maybe he thinks the same way Mike does, that I just danced with him because I'm his friend and I felt sorry for him. How will I ever make him realize how I really feel?*

The dance continued for a few more hours. The band was great, the deejay played all the latest hits during their breaks, and Mr. Willers kept up a lively patter during the awards ceremonies—with prizes for most original costume, weirdest costume, and best costume (Beth and Mike did win that, after all).

But Beth and Adam avoided each other for the rest of the dance. Beth was thinking that Adam just thought of her as a friend, that he only danced with her when he was disgusting-looking, and that when he looked like a movie hero, he wanted to be with Cynthia. Adam was thinking that Beth had only danced with him because she felt sorry for him, not because she really liked him, and that she'd much rather be with the number-one man, Mike Collins, captain of the football team.

The evening that had started out to be so promising for both of them ended with Beth and Adam not even saying good night to each other. Their dates were puzzled by their withdrawn silence on the ride home, and their rather hurried and somewhat reluctant good-night kisses. The Halloween Dance had not fulfilled its promise of a good time for all.

Chapter Six

Monday morning after the Halloween Dance, the hallways were abuzz with gossip, as everyone re-hashed who had danced with whom, what the best costumes *really* were, and on and on.

Cynthia was talking with some of her cheer-leading buddies. "Well, you know, Adam and I got here really early so I could check out the set-up of the dance and everything," she said, "and when Adam went and changed into that costume, I thought I'd just *die*! I mean—ecch!" As usual, Cynthia put her finger down her throat in a mock retch. "Worms! How totally gross. Beth and Adam must be really good friends for her to dance with him in that horrible outfit," Cynthia smiled smugly. "But you know who he danced with when he came back as Adam Gorgeous, don't you? Me!"

Beth was nearby putting her books into her locker, and she overheard Cynthia's entire speech. Beth sighed as she thought to herself, *Cynthia's right. No girl who was interested in Adam as a boyfriend would have danced with him in that disgusting get-up…only a friend would do that.*

Beth smiled at the memory of Cynthia's horrified expression, edging away from Adam as they stood next to the refreshment table. *But it* was *pretty funny, I have to admit—he really freaked Cynthia out.* Beth busied herself fixing her hair and checking out her makeup in her mirror. *I have to remember—Mike paid a lot of attention to me, too. Maybe I should forget about Adam—maybe I'm just kidding myself that I'm really in love with him. It's probably just another one of my crushes.*

Beth tried hard to convince herself, but deep down inside, a little voice kept telling her it wasn't true, that her feelings for Adam were special, and that she couldn't just replace him with Mike Collins, or write him off as just another crush.

Maybe when Adam came back in his new costume and saw me dancing with Mike Collins, Beth thought, *he was jealous, and decided to get my attention by dancing with Cynthia!* Beth smiled at this possibility, then frowned as she realized she had been so upset by the sight of Adam and Cynthia dancing together that she had been unable to use any of her usual flirting tricks to get him back. *It's because I really love him,* she thought. *I just can't play that kind of game with him. On Mike Collins, yes—but on Adam, never. Adam was too special. Besides, Adam would never be jealous of me and some other guy,* she thought sadly. *Why should he—he doesn't love me.*

Beth turned around and found herself staring into Mike Collins's smiling face. He was leaning against the wall of lockers, looking very comfortable. "Hi, Beth," he said. "You must be thinking very heavy thoughts. Your face looked like you were warming up for drama class."

"Oh, hi, Mike. You startled me." Beth looked

down at her toes for a moment. With all her mixed-up feelings about Adam, being this close to Mike always sent her heart racing, just a little. "Great dance Friday, wasn't it?" she said, trying to flirt a little. Beth was still a little embarrassed that she hadn't been more excited about her good-night kiss with Mike.

"Oh sure, terrific," he said. "Once you stopped dancing with the Prince of Worms and started paying some attention to your space explorer, it was wonderful."

Beth looked at Mike curiously. Could he actually be flirting with her? Then again, he was looking like he really meant what he was saying. *Maybe I don't need to flirt so much anymore*, Beth realized with amazement. *Mike actually likes me!*

Cynthia appeared next to the couple. "You and Beth looked gorgeous at the dance," she grinned. "You two really deserved that best costume award."

"Thanks, Cynthia," said Beth, vowing silently that she wouldn't get into some dumb flirting contest with her. "You looked really beautiful, too. And your date didn't look half bad second time around."

"You even seemed to like him when he looked as though he'd risen from the dead. You really are a good friend," said Cynthia, trying to provoke Beth into saying something in front of Mike she might regret. But Beth wouldn't bite.

"You said it yourself, Cynthia," said Beth, as calmly as she could. "Adam and I are real friends."

"Thank heavens for that," said a familiar male voice from behind her. It was Adam, of course. Beth bit her lip. Why did he always appear when she was saying something about them being only friends?

"If it weren't for you," continued Adam, "I would've been an outcast until I reappeared as a swashbuckling hero."

"Well, that's what friends are for," Beth said lightly, trying to make a joke out of it.

"And beautiful princesses are for dancing with, right, Adam?" said Cynthia, taking him by the arm. "It was just an incredible night."

"After I changed costumes, at least," said Adam, his friendly smile taking any cynicism out of his words. "You two looked like you were having a great time," he said somewhat stiffly to Mike and Beth.

Can it be? thought Beth. *Could he really be just a little jealous of Mike and me? It's too much to hope for.*

"I always have a great time," bragged Mike. "That's one of the perks of being captain of the football team, kid. Maybe you'll find out someday," he said, bringing attention to the fact that Adam was a newcomer to both the "in" crowd and football.

Beth was too confused by everything that was being said. Should she try to flirt with Mike and make Adam more jealous? Should she try to compete with Cynthia for Adam's attention? Should she just be sincere with Adam? After all, that's what he said he liked about her. Or should she forget about Adam altogether and just concentrate on Mike? He was a great catch, and he really seemed to be interested in her. *My life is like a soap opera,* Beth moaned to herself.

Fortunately for her, the bell rang and they all had

to go off to their various classes. She would have to worry about it later.

Life as usual went on after the Halloween Dance: classes, homework, cheerleading sessions, football practice, drama-class rehearsals, eating and sleeping and reading and talking—all the everyday things kept rolling by, with no noticeable difference.

Except for Beth—and for Adam, too. Ever since that night at the dance, their relationship had changed: They were no longer quite as comfortable with each other as they had been before. They were a little more distant, maybe even a little cool toward each other. The half-flirting, half-jealous way they behaved in the hallway signaled a change. It was a sign of things to come. Everything at the dance had been so confusing to both of them that their real feelings, which they'd always shared, were now pushed back into some secret hiding place, and only brief glimmers appeared now and again.

Beth tried to convince herself that she didn't really love Adam at all—that it was just another one of her silly crushes, that she had been fooling herself all along. She decided to concentrate on Mike Collins and his apparent interest in her. Adam's new star status must have gone to his head, she thought, and he was now more interested in golden girl Cynthia than his old friend, Beth.

In reality, Adam was kind of overwhelmed by his new popularity, and felt that Beth hadn't changed in her feelings for him at all—but, rather, still thought of him as just a friend. How many times had he heard her say so to Cynthia, even to Mike

Collins? Beth had always been interested in Mike, after all. He must have been dreaming to think that she felt differently about him now. He decided to pay more attention to Cynthia—she was cute, and seemed sweet, and knew all the fun kids in school. And she was always flirting with him. Maybe she really liked him for himself—just because she hadn't given him a whole lot of time last year didn't mean she only liked him for his looks and his football playing. This was a new school year, and maybe she had changed too.

So Beth and Adam stayed apart, separated by thoughts and ideas that kept them from seeing the truth.

Beth managed to keep her cool for quite a while, until Robin finally pulled her aside one day and asked, "What about Adam Brainard, Beth? Anything new happening? You haven't said a thing about him since the Halloween Dance."

And Beth answered, "That's because there's nothing to say, Robin. It was a mistake, that's all."

"A mistake! I've never seen anyone so lovesick over a mistake before in my life! Haven't you told him yet?" Robin had kept her promise not to tell anyone about Beth's secret, and she wanted to know what was going on.

"Tell him what? I've decided to forget about him, Robin," said Beth, trying to convince herself as much as her friend. "Mike Collins is really interested in me, so I might as well go out with him. That makes the most sense to me."

"But Beth," said Robin, concerned for her friend, "when did you ever rely on common sense?

What about your heart? Mike Collins is super-terrific and all that, but he's not the one you want. Don't you remember what you were saying to me before the dance? You've got to tell Adam how you really feel!"

"How can I do that?" said Beth miserably. "I hardly know how I really feel myself. Cynthia's all over Adam every chance she gets, and I keep saying all these dumb things about how Adam and I are just friends—maybe he believes it. He hasn't said anything to me about how much Mike Collins and I are seeing each other. He's probably still just being a 'good friend' and giving me plenty of space to go after the captain of the football team. Adam knows I used to have a terrific crush on him. Adam knows *everything* about me."

She swallowed hard and looked down at her feet. "I've got to be realistic, Robin. I mean, we're in two of my most important classes together, we work together on projects all the time, we see each other across the field at practice nearly every day—if he hasn't seen how I feel up till now, what difference will it make if I say anything or not? Probably he *has* noticed, and he hasn't said anything because he doesn't want to hurt my feelings. I mean, after I went up and danced with him even though he was in that horrible costume, he went off, came back gorgeous, and spent the rest of the night with you-know-who. Isn't that pretty clear? Isn't it obvious to you who he's more interested in?" Beth concluded this monologue with a sigh. "There's no hope for me."

"Oh, Beth," said Robin, groping for something to say to cheer her up. "Don't give up. Maybe

Adam's confused about his feelings too. Maybe he's really jealous of you and Mike, and he just spent the rest of the dance with Cynthia to try and make *you* jealous too!" Robin smiled as she saw Beth look up, a glimmer of hope in her eye. "Don't give up, Beth. Something'll happen, I just know it will. Things seem really mixed up, but they'll get better."

"Maybe, Robin, maybe. But what could happen? Everything's a mess." Beth and Robin looked at each other until the bell rang, and then they ran off to class, with no idea of how to resolve Beth's dilemma.

Beth's next class that day was drama, and she was not looking forward to it. Cynthia had another scene to perform with Adam. Mr. Willers really liked their work together, and had assigned them a particularly difficult scene—two partners in crime, both pretending that they were supporting the other and working together as a team, but in reality keeping secrets and betraying each other.

The trick in acting this kind of scene was that the actors couldn't show two emotions—that of being a true friend and at the same time a cheat—they had to *show* only that they were being true. In their own hearts and minds they had to keep alive the secret betrayal, and somehow that would get across to the audience. Would Adam and Cynthia be able to handle it?

Beth was worried about how the scene would turn out, and she had dropped in at one of their rehearsals. It had been very tense, both of them trying hard to concentrate only on the acting assignment. It was really emotionally draining.

Beth was having a very hard time dealing with

Adam in general. It seemed as if every time they were together—whether in English class, on the practice field after school, in the lunchroom, in drama class, even in the hallways—all their mixed-up thoughts and wishes and desires filled the air with energy. Their feelings were so confused that they had to use every ounce of self-control not to let them show, to spill out and ruin whatever relationship they now had.

But somehow, that day in drama class, everything seemed to come crashing down. Even Beth thought that the scene was awesome: their acting was very real, full of dramatic tension. Both Cynthia and Adam demonstrated their characters' relationship to each other with complete sincerity, making the truth of the characters' betrayal that much more powerful.

Mr. Willers and the rest of the class were silent after this performance. Cynthia and Adam sat on the stage, exhausted, unable to speak, ask a question, or even request criticism. Then, the unheard-of happened: the entire class, including the teacher, broke into solemn applause. Beth's heart almost stopped. Cynthia and Adam looked at each other, wondering if it were some kind of joke; then they looked out at the faces of their classmates and they realized that it was serious. Their work had touched everyone in that room. Cynthia, troubled by the complex emotions the tension-fraught scene had brought up in her, was almost in tears. Beth sat there in shock. *They were good. They were really good,* Beth thought with a sinking feeling.

Mr. Willers broke the applause by speaking: "Well, class, I'm glad to see that everyone has the same reaction I do to this scene. I must tell you all honestly that this is one of the best jobs I've ever seen." He looked at both Cynthia and Adam in turn, to let them see he really meant what he was saying.

"Now, I've been wanting to start preparing for the annual class production," he continued, "and I'm going to hold general auditions for all the roles. But this scene was the best audition piece I could imagine, and I think everyone will agree with my choice for the two leads: Romeo and Juliet will be played by Adam Brainard and Cynthia Jones."

There was a low murmur around the class, but the tone was generally positive—no one objected, not even Beth. *How can I?* thought Beth. *I don't want anyone to know how crushed I am.*

Cynthia was the first to speak. "That's great news. We've worked so well together that I'd like to keep on working with Adam." She looked flushed with happiness.

Adam followed slowly, "If everyone thinks it's fair..." He paused. "Then I'll play the role." He glanced at Beth quickly, then looked down at his hands, folded in his lap. He gave a small, almost undetected, sigh.

Beth's heart felt tired and rumpled. Had she been wrong after all? Did Adam really love her too? Was this only a role for him? She didn't know what to believe. She heard her own voice saying, as if in a dream, "Congratulations, Cynthia. Great job, Adam." And she hoped this dream didn't become a nightmare.

*

As the bell was about to ring to signal the end of the period, everyone crowded around the stage, complimenting Cynthia and Adam on their scene, congratulating them for getting cast in the lead roles, asking them how they made their work so realistic, and so on. Beth felt as if she were in a daze, and she turned to look at Adam to see how he was handling it all. He was looking at her too, even though Cynthia was practically sitting on his lap as she told him how fabulous he was. Beth had an evil thought about how she wished Cynthia would turn into a parakeet or a golden retriever, since that's pretty much the way she always acted around Adam.

Adam reached out his hand, took Beth's hand in it, and gave it a quick, tight squeeze. Beth felt a small warmth beginning to course through her body, counteracting the icy chill she had been experiencing since Mr. Willers's announcement. *This is the worst moment of my life,* thought Beth. The cheerful comments and congratulations of her classmates to Adam and Cynthia drifted past her, creating more chaos that only added to her own confusion.

I could die now. Right here in front of everyone, she thought, then roused herself with a jolt. *What's the matter with me? I have to snap out of this. I'll put my feelings for Adam, this love in my heart, on hold for right now. I have to get on with my life.* Beth's smile of congratulation stretched across her face until she felt her skin would break, and tears welled up behind her eyes. *But I won't cry now,* she thought. *Not here, in front of everyone. Later, when I get home. Then I'll try to figure this all out.*

As they walked out of class and headed toward their lockers, Adam casually put his arm around Beth's shoulder. Luckily, Cynthia was still being swamped by her classmates. "So your old friend did well," Adam said somewhat regretfully. Robin was walking down the hall from the opposite direction, and when she saw them together, her face broke into a grin and she ran up to them.

"I told you something would happen, Beth, didn't I? I just knew it would all work out!" Robin was laughing as she threw her arms around Beth in a big bear hug. Before Robin could do any more damage, Beth cut her off with "Yes, I'm really happy for Adam."

"What's this all about?" asked Adam, curious.

"Oh, I just told Robin I was really nervous for you about your scene for drama class," said Beth, winking furiously at Robin. Beth just couldn't tell Adam how she felt now—but she hoped she could soon. She was still nervous—would he believe her, or would he think it was just another one of her crushes, or worse, that she was like all the other girls, only interested in him for his good looks and new football-star status?

Beth shook her head, got back to the moment. "But don't worry, Robin, it all turned out just fine. Better than I could have imagined." Thankfully, she noticed that Robin was playing along.

"Yeah," said Cynthia, appearing behind them in the hallway. "And get this: Mr. Willers cast Adam and me as Romeo and Juliet in the play. We'll have to have Beth help us with our cues. That'll be some hard work for an old friend, huh?" Robin's face registered her confusion.

"It sure will," said Adam, looking at Beth in a way no "friends" looked at each other. "It sure will."

Robin's not the only one who's confused, Beth thought.

Chapter Seven

Dear Diary:

I don't even know where to begin. You know how miserable and confused I've been ever since the Halloween Dance—well, now I'm even more miserable and confused.

For weeks I've been feeling dumb and dorky around Adam. Well, I wish you could have been there for his scene with Cynthia in drama class. It was incredible! Everyone actually applauded, Diary, can you stand it? Even Mr. Willers! And he said he's decided to cast Cynthia and Adam as the leads...of *ROMEO AND JULIET*!!! Can you believe my luck?

Yes, that's right, Diary, only the most romantic play ever written—tragic too, but all lovers die sooner or later...Romeo and Juliet die for each other, to keep their love pure and untainted by the world and all its miseries. I mean, that's who everyone thinks of when they think of true love, don't they? Romeo and Juliet...Adam and Cynthia. I'm still in shock.

I really was swamped by my feelings today, Diary, I'm not kidding. When Adam reached for my hand right after his scene, I thought, *I could die right now.* I can't believe this is happening to me. I just get finished sinking and I start rising again. Everything is happening too quickly these days. This is no silly crush, Diary, I'm sure of that now—when I had a crush, I'd always be worrying what my friends would think, what I'd wear, where we'd go, or I'd make up fantasies about meeting rock stars or movie actors or whatever. This is really the real thing. Really. Real. This is it.

But how am I going to tell Adam? Will I ever get the courage? Or will I just let all my feelings simmer inside me the way I've been doing all along? I don't know, Diary. I just don't know.

* * *

Dear Diary:

I'm feeling a little overwhelmed by all the things to do: extra studying for final exams in math and science and history and Spanish class; end-of-term papers for Mrs. Griffith's killer English class; working on tumbling routines for the football games (I'm head tumbler in another routine now, too); PLUS rehearsals for *Romeo and Juliet* for Mr. Willers's production—oh yes, Diary, I have more sad news for you.

Can you believe I got cast as the Nurse? The dopiest role in the whole play, and I have to do it. And on top of everything else, I'm the one who's supposed to help Cynthia and Adam (Romeo, that is) get married! Those scenes just kill me. I have to admit, though—I've spent so much time being jealous of Cynthia this term, I never realized what a good actress she is. Maybe being able to say that is a sign that I'm finally starting to sort stuff out, or maybe even grow up a little.

No, I still haven't said anything to Adam about how I feel. Our rehearsal sessions are just that—rehearsals. We don't have any time to sit around talking about anything else—like how we feel. I've never been so busy in my entire life. This term is just incredible: I feel like Alice in Wonderland, running and running and runing as fast as I can just to stay in the same place. And I'll have to run even faster if I want to get anywhere (especially with Adam!).

But I'm not complaining, Diary. I *like* being busy, and things are really exciting most of the time. It seems as though every day is packed with great stuff. Even studying isn't too bad—of course, it's not too good either, but I'm doing pretty well in all my courses, and I'm really even enjoying math (don't you *dare* breathe a word about that to *anyone*!!!). Even Spanish is okay. But the drama-class rehearsals are really tough. I keep feeling as though I'm playing two roles in different levels of the play every time we get together to work on it. My voice says the dialogue for the Nurse. Then my heart repeats Cynthia's words to Adam as Juliet. Wouldn't it be great if Adam were my Romeo? We have big rehearsals for the group scenes, and little rehearsals in twos and threes for the smaller scenes. It's all interesting but very mixed-up for me. Maybe I'll be an actress when I grow up…if I can straighten *this* whole thing out, that is.

Adam's real busy too, of course—he's got a heavy class load, and he's playing first string on the football team. They're doing pretty well so far this season—they might even make the divisional playoffs, if everything keeps going right. Adam's been playing really well too. Sometimes toward the end of a game they know they're going to win, when Mike Collins is a little tired, they even let Adam go in as quarterback. I shriek my lungs out as cheerleader when he does, but I'm sure he can't hear me: he's too busy concentrating on the game. When he gets a chance like that, he can't afford to mess up.

Mike is still real friendly to me, but I'm flirting with him less—there's no time! No, just kidding, Diary, it's not because there's no time. It's because I'm more sure in my own head about my feelings for Adam now, and I don't want anything to get in the way. Even though I haven't told Adam yet I think he knows. (Or does he?) QUIET!

Cynthia still flirts constantly with Adam. She does it every chance she gets in rehearsal. He doesn't encourage her very much, though—he always pretends to be busy with his homework, or another scene, or football plays, or something. (Or maybe he really *is* busy, and if he weren't, he'd be flirting with her as much as ever!) QUIET!!

Enough for now, Diary—I've got to get some sleep so I can get up early and study for that math quiz tomorrow!

* * *

Dear Diary:

Sorry I haven't written for a few days—you know how busy I've been. Actually you *don't* know how busy I've been. Can you believe that Mike Collins asked me out to a movie tonight, and I turned him down because I have to work on this paper for Mrs. Griffith?! If you asked me last year would I turn down Mike Collins for *ANY REASON WHATSOEVER*, I would tell you never, no way, forget it, what are you, crazy? But my time is so tight these days, every minute is scheduled. It has to be, Diary, or I'll never get everything done.

I'll tell you one thing, though: I turned down Mike in the middle of the hallway, and Adam heard everything—he was standing right behind me. I'd swear I saw him smile afterwards. Maybe he's beginning to figure out that I'm not hung up on Mike Collins. And I think he's been acting a little cooler toward Cynthia too—kind of like he's trying to tell me I shouldn't stay away from him so he can go out with her or something.

Oh, life is so crazy right now. We're starting to prepare our costumes and stuff for the *Romeo and Juliet* production—Cynthia has these fabulous velvet gowns, in luscious colors like forest green, burgundy, and royal blue, with trims of gold braid and pearl beading and stuff. Meanwhile, poor Beth! I'm playing the fat old Nurse, so they're stuffing my costume to make me look like a sack of potatoes! I'd have a hard time flirting with anyone in that outfit. I can't imagine why any leading man would choose a dowdy old nurse over a beautifully dressed medieval heroine. Oh well, I can hope. Or can I?

* * *

Dear Diary:

Rehearsal today was just UNBELIEVABLE!!! Adam and Cynthia were working on the second balcony scene—the one where they leave Juliet's bedroom after the wedding night—and I suddenly heard the lines they probably had been reciting by themselves for days:

ROMEO: Farewell, farewell! one kiss and I'll descend.
JULIET: Art thou gone so? my lord, my love, my friend!

Suddenly, I felt as if *I* had answered Adam as Juliet. In my fantasy, I guess I was so trembly and tingly from that kiss that I heard the words as if for the first time—"My lord, my love, my friend"...MY FRIEND!!! I wanted to leap up in the air and tell everyone that my love for Adam has blossomed out of our friendship. It's not something new, some strange development: it's a natural progression, right and good and beautiful. Luckily, I realized that I was daydreaming before I embarrassed myself and everyone around me. I stepped back into my role as the Nurse, wondering if I'll ever be anyone else.

I seem to be thinking more than ever these days —all this studying and working and practice has revved up my brain cells, and I can't get them to slow down. I'm seeing everything differently: analyzing my whole world, my whole life, every day as I live through it. I've never felt like this before, Diary, but I kind of like it. I'm not some brainhead or anything—I just find myself wondering about everything and everyone, and why things are the way they are. I'll drift off into dreams now, Diary, and hopefully I'll find some answers there.

* * *

Dear Diary:

I am ready to scream!!! I overheard Cynthia talking with another girl in our drama class today: the other girl was saying she thought Adam and Cynthia must really be good actors to play Romeo and Juliet so realistically. Cynthia replied that she had heard that every time an actor and actress play Romeo and Juliet, they begin to fall a little in love. "Adam and I passed that point many rehearsals ago," Cynthia confidently stated. Diary, that can't be true. I *know* it's just the old story of the actor falling in love with the *role* the actress is playing, and vice versa. ARGHHH! If she says anything like that to me— or to Adam—I'll just die...or I'll kill her!!! (Or both.)

* * *

Dear Diary:

History exam today—blecch! I probably didn't do too well on it: it was all dates and causes of war in Europe. I can't think of anything more boring, more horrible, than studying war. The only conceivable reason for it is what our history teacher said at the beginning of term: "Those who cannot remember the past are condemned to repeat it." She said it was a quote from some famous person (I forget who), and it's the only thing that keeps me awake when I'm reading those boring history textbooks (who writes those things anyway?).

I'm exhausted. Cheered my lungs and legs and everything out this afternoon at the football game: It was the final match in the semi-finals, and Hampstead High won! We're going into the divisional playoffs this month, and we're all really excited. I'm sure it's our great cheering that makes the guys want to win! Got to sleep. Bye.

* * *

Dear Diary:

Today Adam and Cynthia rehearsed the scene where Romeo and Juliet first meet at the masked ball. Well, when it came to the part about the kiss —you know, when Romeo touches Juliet, and then goes on about how if his hands are too rough, his lips are soft, and—oh, I hate to remember it, but I'll just write it out for you:

ROMEO: If I profane with my unworthiest hand
This holy shrine, the gentle fine is this,
My lips, two blushing pilgrims, ready stand
To smooth that rough touch with a tender kiss.

Well, it goes on from there, more and more, each of them flirting with the other (I guess times haven't changed so much, after all) until they kiss…and what a kiss! Diary, I thought I'd faint: Adam seems to be so tender, so gentle, so loving… Why can't I be Juliet?

I hope it's just because he's a great actor and is playing the part of Romeo exactly as it should be played. No. I know, I just know it's because he's pretending that I'm really Juliet. I almost said something to him today after rehearsal, but I just couldn't. Why can't I stop wanting to be Juliet? Maybe I should try to stop wanting Adam, period. Is it just that every Juliet falls in love with her Romeo? Wait a minute—I'm not even Juliet! But I've got to tell him, Diary, I've just got to. Or else my heart will burst—"Ay, me!" (That's from the play.) "Good night, good night! As sweet repose and rest/Come to thy heart as that within my breast!…My bounty is as boundless as the sea,/My love as deep; the more I give to thee,/The more I have, for both are infinite… dear love, adieu!…A thousand times good night!" Yes, dear Diary, I know I'm being even more dramatic than usual, but how else can I act when my heart is breaking?

Chapter Eight

As the end of term approached, all the students' lives became more hectic as they rushed to complete assignments and prepare for exams. The football team—and the cheerleaders—especially felt the crunch, for Hampstead High had made it to the finals, and there were extra practices scheduled to get the players into top form.

Beth raced all over to fit her activities into the short, cold winter days. She muddled through her history, Spanish, and science finals, concentrating more on English and math—and, of course, on cheerleading practice and rehearsals for *Romeo and Juliet*. She read the play over and over until its language and poetry had almost become a part of her, even though she still felt frustrated at playing the dowdy old Nurse.

Adam was also hustling a lot to keep up with all his stuff. Since he was pretty new to football, his free time was taken up studying plays and strategies—as well as toning and strengthening his muscles, and trying to become more aggressive on the field. He knew that real jocks talked tough, acted tough, and played tough. Between classes and homework and football and play rehearsals, he barely had time for anything else—including paying a lot of attention to all the girls in his class, who were flirting more and more with the new hunk in their midst.

In addition to rehearsals, Cynthia kept trying to get more of Adam's time, but with almost no success. She would stop him after drama class to get his opinion on how she should do a particular scene, or run up to him after football practice to tell him how great he was doing, but Adam would always politely cut her off by saying, "I'm sorry, Cynthia, but I've got to go [study, practice, rehearse, whatever]." Cynthia always looked disappointed.

Even Mr. Cool himself, Mike Collins, felt the pressure. He was leading the Hampstead High football team in a winning season, and he really wanted them to win the divisional championship. As captain of the team, he always managed to squeak by on his exams, usually by accepting help from brainy girls, or by sweet-talking the teacher, or by having the coach send them a note about "his importance to the team and school spirit"—blah blah blah—but even so, his workload was heavier than usual and he walked the halls with a tense expression on his handsome face. He continued to flirt with Beth, and was kind of puzzled by her seeming indifference to him, but wrote it off to the fact that he wasn't really pursuing her with all his energy and charm—and that she, too, had a full schedule at this time of year.

Robin had finally spilled the beans about Beth's feelings for Adam to a couple of their close friends on the cheerleading squad. Most of them, just as Beth suspected, said, "Oh, it's just another one of

Beth's crushes. She'll forget about him soon, just like all the others." One noted, "Beth never liked Adam like that before—it must be because he's such a hunk this year." Another asked, "Why doesn't she go after Mike Collins? He really likes her this year."

And when Cynthia overheard these conversations, she would repeat, "It's just because she's in the play. She sees us playing Romeo and Juliet all the time and she hates being the Nurse. Wanting to be Juliet has really gone to her head. It's all an illusion—she'll get over it when the production is finished."

Robin tried to vouch for her friend's sincerity, but the other girls just laughed. "Beth's always going ga-ga over some guy or another," they'd say. "She'll get over Adam Brainard as soon as the next hunk appears on the scene."

But Kate Morris seemed to understand. She had always been Beth's good friend, and she could see something different in Beth this year. "I think it's just terrific, Beth. You've always been friends with Adam—I'm not going to tease you about having a crush on him. Don't pay attention to what everyone else says. If you like him, that's all that matters."

Beth looked at Kate curiously: her friend had never been so sensitive before. Kate was usually the queen of the "in" crowd, and always played hard to get with guys. Beth decided Kate must be going through some changes herself.

"But what if Adam thinks it's just another crush —I mean, he knows everything about me, Kate! I can't fool him." Beth was looking for some more support from her friend.

Kate happily supplied it. "I know you can't fool

him, Beth. So, if I can see it's different than all those other guys, so will Adam! Seriously, I believe you—really, I do. Your feelings for him have changed, so follow up on it." Kate smiled her big cheerleader grin. "When are you going to tell him how you feel?"

Beth smiled at her friend warmly. "I don't know, Kate. Everything is just so crazy these days. I don't want to distract him before the big game this weekend, and I keep worrying that if I tell him and he doesn't feel the same way, I'll be so heartbroken I'll *never* be able to act like Juliet to his Romeo, even if I ever have the chance. Right now, it's all so romantic and exciting, hearing the words of the play. I want to have the words just fly from *my* lips as if I had written them myself, but then, there I am—the Nurse. And *Cynthia* is Juliet instead. And...and..." Beth stuttered in her nervousness, unable to complete her sentence.

"Oh, Beth," said Kate, "you're still thinking this is just another crush—you've got to believe *yourself* that it's something different. Telling him won't change things, not when you really feel this way. I mean, playing hard to get is good for a while, but once it's serious, you've got to let the guy know where you stand."

"I know, Kate, I know. And I will...soon." Beth bit her lip. "Real soon."

Fortunately for Beth, at that moment their cheerleading coach called them out on the field to practice, so she didn't have to make any commitment to Kate—or to herself—about when she was going to talk to Adam about her feelings for him. *Soon,* thought Beth, as they started their warm-ups, *real soon.*

Somehow, they all made it through the week, attending classes, handing in papers, taking quizzes and exams—and coffee—and making it to practice and rehearsals and everything else. Beth decided she wasn't going to say anything to Adam until after the playoff—after all, if he wasn't making the first move, why should she? Finally, the weekend of the big game arrived, and the whole school was really up for it: The football team felt confident, and the cheerleaders were ready to cheer them on to victory.

The turnout for the game was huge. Hampstead High usually had pretty good student and local attendance at its games, and this year it had done better than usual, since it had such a winning team. Now, for the playoff, the stands were nearly filled. There was a light snow falling, and it was clear it was going to be a tough game for all the players.

Beth and the other cheerleaders ran out onto the field to start their pre-game warm-ups, and the crowd let out a huge cheer of approval. Beth and Robin scanned the seats, wide-eyed at the number of people. All the girls had taken extra time primping before the game, and they looked great—every hair in place, all their uniforms pressed and perfect. Their energy was high: They really wanted their guys to win.

When the Hampstead High Vikings ran onto the field, the crowd's cheer turned into a roar. Every member of the team received wild applause, and the guys went into their huddle excited and ready to play. The opposing team, from nearby Mayview High, also had a lot of fans in the stands, and they got equally big cheers as they ran onto the field.

The game began, and everyone yelled and cheered, no one more than the Hampstead High cheering squad. Beth jumped, kicked, shouted, and screamed her best. She wanted Hampstead to get a big lead early, so that maybe Adam would get a chance to play quarterback in this big final game.

But she didn't get her wish. By half time, the score was tied at 6-all, and it was clear it was going to be a close game. Both teams were looking good and playing hard.

As the second half began, Beth concentrated on leading her two routines, so she had to pay less attention to the game. But suddenly, a loud cry went up from the audience, and the cheerleaders stopped to see what had happened. Mike Collins, quarterback and captain of the team, was lying in the middle of the field!

Apparently, one of the opposing players had tackled Mike around his knees and really hit him hard. His left knee was injured—sprained and maybe worse—and it was clear he was going to have to sit out the rest of the game.

Beth's face darkened with concern for the team— then brightened as she realized this might be Adam's big chance. *Oh please*, she thought, *oh please, let them send Adam in as quarterback. I mean, I hope Mike's not hurt bad or anything, but if Adam could play—and win—oh, what a chance for him!!* She turned back to the other cheerleaders and said, "Okay, guys, we've really got to turn it on now. They've got to keep going! We've got to win!"

The other girls looked skeptical, and comments like "How can we win without Mike?" floated around. But Beth started the next routine with extra energy, and the other girls followed along. It was everyone's time to be a winner.

After Mike was carried off the field to wild applause for his playing, and his courage, the Hampstead High team ran off to confer with their coach during the time-out.

Then a whistle blew, and Beth looked up for an anxious few seconds to see who was on the team. Her eyes took in the huddle and she picked out Adam's back before she spotted his number. He was in now as quarterback during one of the most important games of the year. *Oh, Adam, I love you! You've got to do it!* She doubled her cheering efforts, and the squad nearly glowed from the energy they were putting out to encourage their team to victory.

The rest of the game was straight out of a happy storybook. Adam's choice of plays sent the Mayview team reeling, and his confidence inspired the other members of the Hampstead High team to play their very best. Adam also got off two perfect passes, and carried the ball in himself for the winning touchdown. Even the snow on the ground couldn't stop the Hampstead Vikings from running to a resounding victory.

The crowd in the stands went wild for their new hero, screaming, "AD-AM, AD-AM, BRAIN-ARD, BRAIN-ARD!" Beth and the other cheerleaders picked up the cry, and the stadium rocked with the sound of Adam's name as his teammates picked him up and carried him off the field on their shoulders.

Adam went straight to the medic's area, to see how Mike was doing. "You did great, kid," Mike said, smiling through his pain. "I couldn't have done better myself... well, maybe just a little better." Mike and Adam laughed, no hard feelings about what had happened—they were going to be real friends.

The cheerleaders then swarmed the team, followed closely by family, friends, and fans, all of them trying to get to Adam. There were cries of "Great work, Adam!" "Didn't know you had it in you!" "Outstanding, Brainard, outstanding!" And so on. Cynthia pushed her way through the crowd, threw her arms around Adam, and planted a big kiss right on his mouth. Everyone went "Ooooh," and Cynthia laughed, kissing him again. When that happened, Beth wished that a hole would open on the playing field for her to crawl into.

Beth hung back, smiling, so happy for her old friend—so proud of him. But she didn't want to intrude on his moment. She wanted him to feel all the glory of being the quarterback who won the all-important final game of the championship. Another trophy for Hampstead High, and Adam had led the team to victory! She was nearly crying with happiness and love for Adam.

But Adam was scanning the faces, searching for Beth across the huge crowd—and he found her. A broad smile spread across his face, and he called out, still breathless from the game, "I can't believe it."

Adam finally reached her. "Oh, Adam," cried Beth, unable to contain herself any longer, "you were wonderful, just wonderful! I knew you could do it, I knew you could. You just needed the chance to prove it to everyone else—and did you ever prove it today!"

The two embraced each other in a tight hug, both still wet and out of breath from their activity on the playing field, and everyone around them cheered. Beth whispered in Adam's ear, "How on earth did you do it, Adam? With so much pressure, everyone watching—how?"

And Adam whispered back, even more softly, so that no one could hear, "When the time came to make the play, it was like everything was changing. I had a chance to stop being the Prince of Worms and turn into the adventurer again. I looked over and there you were, cheering your heart out. And I realized that you would always cheer for me—no matter who I am or what I do."

Adam gazed at Beth, and then they both kissed quickly before they were overtaken by the shouting, hooting, screaming crowd that surrounded them both. Beth's sense of contentment flipped back into her normal state of confusion as Adam added over his shoulder, "I feel really great that I can count on you as my best friend."

Dear Diary:

It's only been the most incredible day in my entire life...(I think). I don't know how I can possibly write it all down.

First of all, Hampstead won the championship —and the star of the game was Adam Brainard! He was terrific, and everyone just went wild over him.

Well, afterwards, of course, he was mobbed, but he searched me out in the crowd and gave me a

97

big hug…and then started telling me everything I ever wanted to hear him say. And just when I figured that he loved me, he told me that he was glad I was his friend. Everyone around us was yelling and cheering, and we didn't get to say any more. It was just an incredible day, Diary. Unbelievable, amazing, marvelous, wonderful— well, you get the idea. And let's not forget—confusing. I can't decide whether I'll always be the Nurse, or maybe Adam is starting to think of me as his Juliet.

Afterwards, the football team and all the cheerleaders went out for pizza and stuff, and we all sat around talking and laughing and telling jokes, and replaying the game over and over again. And Adam sat next to me the whole time. I know it's time for me to tell him how I feel, Diary, but I still don't quite dare. I mean, what if he really only thinks of me as a friend? Was he just excited because he was the hero of the playoff? All right, but what if he's only being romantic *because* he's Romeo and he's used to being romantic? Won't it all come to an end after football season and the production? Oh, Diary, everything is almost perfect, but I still feel totally confused and jumbled up inside. Will it always be like this?

I guess I just won't know what's going on for real until after the drama-class production. *Then* we'll be able to sort out dreams from reality. And speaking of that production—it's next week, and I am more nervous than ever! Because Adam was such a star today, the auditorium is sure to be PACKED—all of Adam's fans will be there to see their hero as Romeo. What if I mess up, like forget my lines, or trip on my costume's stuffing, or get the hiccups or something? Robin and Kate tell me it's normal to get stage fright, that all great actresses get it before they go onstage in a really important production—but I don't know. And, besides, who says I'm a great actress? Every time I think about the play, my stomach gets twisted into knots and my hands start sweating. Is this what it means to be an actress? It's almost as hard as being in love. I'm not sure that I want to be either!

Chapter Nine

Beth's last hurdle of the term was in sight. She had taken all of her exams, handed in all her final papers, cheered the football team (and Adam) on to victory in the championship—now all she had to do was live through the drama-class production of *Romeo and Juliet. Not just live through it,* she thought, *but really DO it, actually get onstage in front of hundreds of people and somehow touch them by bringing my character to life.* It was a tough challenge, but Beth wanted to meet it. So did everyone else in the production.

Mr. Willers was really encouraging to her, and to the whole class. "I know you can do it, kids," he would say, over and over again. "We've been working hard all term, and I have confidence in you. Cynthia and Adam—just keep up the good work you've been doing up till now and you'll have no problems. I really think this production can be something special." His direction of the actors in each of the scenes was sensitive and helpful. He got the students to bring out special aspects of their characters, and to add something to the play as a whole.

Robin was stage manager for the production, and Beth confided in her backstage before the final dress rehearsal, "Robin, I have never been more nervous in my entire life. Remember all those crushes I used to have, and how crazy I'd go over one guy or another? Well, all of that was EASY compared to this."

"So think of all the experience you've had at being nervous," said Robin, trying to cheer her friend up. "You're an expert! Seriously, though, you really haven't got anything to be nervous about —you and Adam have been getting more and more involved all term long. I've heard about your scenes as the Nurse from some of the other kids in drama class. They all say you're really amazing. That's not a glamorous part, and you're doing a great job."

"I know," said Beth worriedly, "and that makes me even more nervous! I mean, everyone expects so much of us..."

"Oh, come on, Beth—no one is expecting you to be Broadway stars or anything. Just do the best you can, and everyone will be happy." Robin looked at her friend closely. "I think I know why you're really nervous, Beth. It's because after this production you'll have no more excuses not to tell Adam how you really feel about him. The moment of truth is coming."

Beth looked down at her hands, nervously clutched in her lap, and Robin knew she had hit the nail on the head. She continued, "Of course, I don't know why that should make you nervous either—the way Adam treated you after the big game, I don't think you'll have any problems at all." She gave Beth a big smile.

Beth gave her a weak smile back and said, "I

know, Robin, I know—it's just that...well, being up onstage in the play is exciting, but in real life... it's all just kind of overwhelming, that's all," she ended weakly. She didn't have the heart to add how frustrating it had also been for her.

"Well, you'll have to worry about it later, kid, because that was your cue—now get out there and be brilliant!" Robin said firmly, pushing Beth in the direction of the stage. "Break a leg!" she called after her in a loud whisper.

Adam was nervous too, in his own quiet way. The excitement he'd created by leading the school to victory in the championship had only just begun to subside, and he was still floored by the attention and admiration he'd received from all his fellow students because of what he had done. But Adam didn't have anyone he could talk to about how confused he felt. Beth had always been his confidante, but their relationship had changed so much over the past few months that he certainly didn't feel comfortable talking to her about these things— especially since his new feelings for her confused him most of all. So he turned to someone else he felt he just might be able to talk to.

The day before, Adam had gone to visit Mike Collins at home, where he was laid up with a big cast on his leg—fortunately, he had just sprained his knee, not broken it, but he was still pretty much immobilized by the accident. Adam had felt a sudden closeness with Mike on the football field after the big game, when they shook hands and Mike said, "You did great, kid." Maybe, just maybe, he'd be able to tell Mike his feelings about the play—and about Beth.

"How you doing, champ?" Mike called out as Adam entered his room. Mike was sitting up in his bed, his cast out from under the blankets so that Adam could see all the signatures and pictures his friends had drawn on it: "We love you, Mike," "Get well soon, Tiger," and so on.

"Pretty good, Mike, I guess," said Adam, sitting down in a chair by the bed.

"You guess? Replacement quarterback leads Hampstead High Vikings to stunning victory, and he only *guesses* he's pretty good? What gives, kid?"

Adam looked at Mike, and saw that his friendly face was filled with concern. He opened up to him right away: "It's this play, Mike. *Romeo and Juliet.* We go on tomorrow, and—well, I'm nervous."

"Nervous?" Mike cut him off with a snort. "You? After what you went through last week—and pulled off perfectly, I might add—I'd think you'd never get nervous about *anything. I'm* the one who ought to be nervous—that you might replace me as quarterback!"

"Oh, come on, Mike," said Adam modestly. "You've got no competition from me—I'm a newcomer to the game. But I'm new to this acting stuff too. I mean, Cynthia and I have been doing pretty well all term, but—"

"But what?" said Mike. "Just keep on doing the same thing. Don't let the audience distract your attention from the job you've got to do. It's just like being on the football field: they're all screaming and shouting, and all these gorgeous cheerleaders are jumping up and down and calling your name, and you've got to focus—I mean, *completely focus*

104

yourself—on the game, on that little inflated piece of pigskin. I'm sure acting's just the same thing," he concluded confidently.

"Maybe," said Adam uncertainly. "But it's that much harder when one of the gorgeous cheerleaders is playing in one of the supporting roles—and you're really in love with *her,* but speaking romantic lines to another Juliet."

Mike studied Adam's face seriously. "Beth—you mean Beth Patterson? Oh gosh, Adam, you mean you're really in love with her? You sure you're not just getting carried away with this Romeo thing?"

"No, Mike," Adam said softly. "It's for real. But I don't know how to tell her. I mean—first of all, I think she really likes you."

"Me! Hah!" snorted Mike. "Last year, maybe. I couldn't get rid of her. But this year, I've kinda been going after her—not too seriously, of course, but a little—and except for one movie and that Halloween Dance, she's barely paid any attention to me at all. You're not my competition only on the football team—you're my competition with girls too!" Mike laughed at his own words, realizing that even with Adam's new height and good looks, Mike was still the "big man on campus."

"Now you're really kidding me, Mike," Adam said, "and I'm serious."

"What are you so serious about? Just play the love scenes with Cynthia like you really mean 'em, but take Beth out afterwards and tell her it wasn't Romeo saying those lines to Juliet; it was you saying them to her, Beth Patterson." Mike smiled at Adam's worried expression. "Come on, kid, lighten up. You two have been friends forever. If it doesn't work out, you can go back to being friends, can't you?"

"I don't know, Mike," said Adam quietly. "And I guess that scares me a little too. Beth was always the one I could confide in."

"So confide in her now, dummy! Tell her how you feel. Listen, I think she's great, really, and I wish you all the luck in the world. Besides, maybe if you two start going out, Cynthia will stop hanging all over you and start paying some more attention to me again." The two boys smiled at each other, and clasped hands in a gesture of friendship.

"Thanks, Mike," said Adam sincerely.

"Don't thank me," said Mike. "Just put on a good show. They're going to wheel me in to the front row, and I want to have a good time, not be bored to death for two hours. Just be yourself, kid! It'll all work out."

Adam had left Mike's house feeling a little better, more confident—but now, backstage before dress rehearsal, his nervousness had come back. He hadn't even mentioned to Mike the fact that his audience would be bigger—and expecting more of him—because of his performance on the football field the week before. Adam heard the cue for his first entrance: "Could we but learn from whence his sorrows grow, / We would as willingly give cure as know." *How appropriate*, he thought to himself, as he walked out onto the stage.

The dress rehearsal was awful: props broke, set pieces didn't work, the actors sounded false and stilted. Everyone got more and more nervous from all the mishaps, and they were convinced the production was going to be a disaster.

Mr. Willers sat in the audience with a big grin, noticing how worried all the kids were. "Come on, come on, everybody. Cheer up. It's an old theater tradition: A bad dress rehearsal means a good opening night. Don't worry so much! It's all going to be just fine."

Everyone mumbled and grumbled, and one stagehand said, "Well, if that old saying is true, this is going to be the greatest opening night in history."

And it was. From the moment the audience first entered the theater, everything went just perfectly. The actors peered out through the curtains before the start of Act One, gaping at the full house, then running off backstage to report to their friends and make last-minute costume adjustments.

Everything worked right: the props held up, the stage set didn't fall down, the actors didn't trip over their costumes or forget their lines. Beth's performance as the Nurse got roars of laughter from the audience, and Cynthia and Adam, in their few scenes together as the young lovers, clearly touched the entire audience. There were sniffles to be heard at the final death scene, and a tear or two was hurriedly wiped away from various faces in the audience.

The evening seemed beyond perfect: it was magical. The tragic story of Romeo and Juliet was uplifted by the stars' performances, and in the final scene, when Romeo's father states he will raise a golden statue to honor Juliet's love, and Juliet's father says he will do the same for Romeo, it seemed as if the two lovers themselves were transformed into gold, becoming eternal symbols of true love.

When the last lines were spoken, "For never was a story of more woe/Than this of Juliet and her Romeo," the curtain fell to thunderous applause, and the entire cast joined together to take their curtain calls. As the curtain rose again, Adam could see Mike in the front row, his leg propped up on another chair, giving Adam a big grin and a thumbs up sign.

The curtain fell after the general company bows, but the applause continued, so Cynthia and Adam took a curtain call, just the two of them. The volume of the applause rose even higher, and shouts of "Bravo! Bravo!" were heard throughout the house. The curtain fell again, but still the applause continued, so the company gathered once again, joined hands, and took a bow as the curtain rose one final time.

Adam kept holding Cynthia's hand after this final curtain call, and the two of them stood there in the middle of the stage, just looking at each other.

This is just too much for me to bear, thought Beth sorrowfully. *I've got to get out of here, get this padding off me, and go and hide. How could I have ever thought I could be anything more than the Nurse?*

Suddenly, she felt someone grab her arm. She turned around slowly, thinking, *If this were a play, then this would be my leading man come to claim me—but my play is over.*

It was Adam. As she searched his eyes, Beth was amazed to hear him say, "It was a sad story for Romeo and Juliet." He added softly, "But it doesn't have to be for us. As I said each line tonight, and in all the rehearsals, I was saying them to you in my heart. You've always been my *only* Juliet."

108

"Oh, Adam," said Beth, holding her gaze on Adam's eyes. "I've been wanting to tell you for so long...I love you, Adam. I love you with all my heart."

Adam looked at Beth, not believing his good fortune. Could so many good things happen to one person in one week's time? "I love you too, Beth. I have for a long time. I just didn't know how to tell you either."

Then they kissed again, but this kiss was greater than all the ones in the play, or in rehearsals, or after the championship football game. Beth smiled because she knew. Now she really knew. *I'll never say "only friends" again*, she thought. *We're friends and much, much more.*

The rest of the cast crowded around the kissing couple, and a big "OOOOoooh!" went up from them all. Adam and Beth stopped their kiss, looked at all their friends, and smiled, blushing a little.

"So, the real Romeo and Juliet have gotten together, after all—nothing could keep them apart!" joked Cynthia, having the grace to be a good loser.

"Well, kids," said Mr. Willers, "you did great. I don't think there was a dry eye in the house. Really, you did even better than I had any right to expect—all of you," he concluded, turning his head to look at every member of the cast.

Family and friends from the audience started to come backstage, and all the cast members were surrounded by people congratulating them on their performances, hugging them, slapping them on the back, and so on. Adam and Beth, along with everyone else, smiled, shook hands, and murmured thank you a thousand times, but they kept looking over at each other, neither one of them quite believing that their dreams had at last come true.

Robin and Kate grabbed Beth from out of the center of a circle of well-wishers and dragged her off backstage.

"Tell us all about it," begged Kate, "and don't leave out a single detail."

"I saw him kiss you again after that last curtain call, Beth—come on, tell all. That wasn't in the script. I ought to know. I was the stage manager, after all," teased Robin.

"Oh, you guys," said Beth, blushing. "It's all so amazing. I think Adam really loves me too!"

"You see?" said Kate. "I told you you were silly to be worried about it. You should have told him ages ago."

"Oh no," said Beth, "then this night wouldn't have been so absolutely perfect. Sometimes, if you wait, it's even better. I guess that's something new for me to say, huh? But it's true."

"Oh, Beth, how exciting!" said Robin. "I'm so happy for you. And your performance was great too."

"It really was, Beth," said Kate admiringly. "The whole play was great. I was actually crying at the end, I swear, I really was."

"It was really incredible," said Beth, bubbling over with happiness. "We all worked so hard on this play that when it actually came time to do it, it seemed easy."

The three friends stood there smiling at each other, until Mr. Willers clapped his hands and announced, "All right, crew, let's get cleaned up and out of here! We've got to be out of this theater by eleven at the latest—and everyone's invited to the pizza parlor for a cast party!"

A cheer went up from all the students, and they all started rushing around, changing clothes, washing off stage makeup, taking down sets, and so on. Everyone wanted to relax and congratulate everyone else for the terrific production.

Adam came to the girls' dressing room when he had changed, and waited for Beth to appear. When she came out the door, Adam handed her a huge bouquet of flowers.

"Oh my," she said, inhaling their fragrance. "Where did you get these?"

"I kept them hidden during the performance," said Adam, smiling. "I think they might be a little wilted by now."

"Oh no, they're perfect!" sighed Beth. "Perfect. Just like you..." They stood looking at each other in silence.

Then Adam took Beth's hand. "You'll walk with me to the cast party, won't you?" he asked.

"How could Juliet refuse her Romeo?" replied Beth flirtatiously. "I'd love to," she said more seriously, twining her fingers through his.

They walked together to the pizza parlor, where the entire cast greeted them with cheers. Mr. Willers again congratulated them all on their hard work throughout the term and their excellent performances that night. Both Beth and Adam were ecstatic —filled with the happiness of the night.

Adam walked Beth home after the party, and kissed her good night in front of the door to her house. Beth felt her heart fluttering, but deep inside there was a calm sense of rightness about her and Adam finally being together.

"Good night, sweet Juliet—sweet Beth," said Adam, kissing her once more, lightly, on the lips.

"Good night, dear Romeo, dear Adam—my lord, my love, my friend."

Dear Diary:

All my dreams have come true, at last. I can't believe how lucky I am. In some ways, I feel silly I didn't tell Adam I loved him earlier...but in some ways, I'm glad I waited, like I told Robin and Kate. Tonight was just the absolute best night of my life.

The play was a complete success, and after the last curtain call, everything was magic. Adam said he loved me too, and had for a long time—he'd been afraid to tell me too! Can you believe it, Diary? I almost pinched myself to make sure I wasn't dreaming.

I can't wait for Christmas break—Adam and I are going to see each other almost every day. I still can't believe that an old friend could become a true love!

Good night, Diary, good night—as Romeo said, "O blessed, blessed night! I am afeard,/Being in night, all this is but a dream..." But it's not a dream, Diary, for tomorrow I'll wake up, and Adam and I are going to celebrate with lunch at the coffee shop! What could be more down-to-earth than that?

Chapter Ten

Dear Diary:

Christmas break is turning out to be just as wonderful as I had hoped. After Adam and I had lunch, we went down to the pond and went ice-skating together—holding hands the whole time, and helping each other up if one of us fell. (I loved falling today, Diary, because then he'd have to put his arms around me, and I could feel his strong arms and shoulders as he'd help me get back on my feet.)

Afterwards, we went back to the coffee shop for hot chocolate, and we sat and talked for hours, just like old times, only better, because we were talking about *us*! I can't believe this is really happening to me.

Dear Diary:

Yet another wonderful day: Adam and I went to the movies, and then for a walk in the park. The movie was great, and the walk was really romantic—well, at least it started out that way. But as we were walking, we came across a bunch of little kids sledding down the hill on all sorts of things—round metal saucers, cardboard boxes, wooden sleds—everything. Well, Adam and I decided to join them, and we had a ball! We went rolling down the hill, sliding down the hill, climbing back up, gasping for breath, covered with snow, laughing until we fell in a heap... and then it got romantic again, as we sat there in the snow, kissing each other. I can still remember the snowflakes clinging to his long, dark lashes. I don't want to sleep because I don't want to stop thinking about all of this. Good night, Diary. Every night seems to be a good one now!

Dear Diary:

Robin had a Christmas party for all the kids at her house this afternoon, and it was really great! Everyone was there—Kate, and Jamie Thompson, and Robin, of course, and Cynthia, and even Mike Collins, still in that big leg cast. Adam and I went together, and we signed Mike's cast, "With love from the real Romeo and Juliet"—I think he got quite a kick out of that (no pun intended).

Adam and I danced together about a thousand times, each one more wonderful than the last. I can't believe I love him more every time I see him. This is definitely different than anything I've ever felt before in my life.

One more thing: Cynthia isn't flirting with Adam anymore, and Mike isn't flirting with me anymore—they're both flirting with each other! How does that grab you, Diary? Wouldn't that turn out to be just perfect: if Mike and Cynthia got together the way Adam and I have gotten together? I'm so happy, I want everyone to be happy right along with us!!!

* * *

Dear Diary:

Went shopping for last-minute Christmas gifts
with Kate and Robin today—the stores were absolutely MOBBED!!! Why do people all put off
their shopping until the last minute? I mean, I
had to, because I didn't know I was going to
have a super-terrific boyfriend like Adam to buy
Christmas presents for...surely *everyone* can't
have fallen in love in the last two weeks?!

Anyway, I hope Adam likes his present.

* * *

Dear Diary:

Tonight Adam and I and Robin and Kate and
Jamie Thompson all went out caroling in the
snow! We had so much fun, even if Robin really
can't carry a tune.

First we walked all the way up Maple Street,
just laughing and joking and stuff. Then we
started walking back, slowly, singing carols as
we came, going down all the little side streets.
People came to their front doors as we passed,
and smiled and waved and stuff. Mrs. Johnson
over on Elm Street even invited us in for hot
chocolate! It was just a beautiful evening.

"Come on, let's walk to your house," Adam said as he took Beth's hand and tucked it inside his pocket.

It was Christmas Eve and Beth was dying to tell him about his present, but he'd see it soon enough. She wondered if he'd gotten her anything, but Beth felt so sure and happy about Adam that she realized "if" wasn't the right word. She *knew* in her heart he had.

No one was home when Beth and Adam pushed open the front door, and Beth was grateful for the stillness. She snuggled against Adam's strong shoulder and felt warmer than she ever had in her life.

Adam gently pushed away. "I have a present for you." He reached into his pocket and pulled out a small blue box.

Beth's eyes widened. She was dying to see what was inside, but she had to wait. "Just a second. I've got something too. Wait. Wait," she called over her shoulder as she raced up the stairs. She was back in a minute with a small rectangular package.

"You go first," she said as she gently put the tissue-wrapped gift in Adam's hand.

"What is it?"

"Open it," she said eagerly.

It was a small leather-bound volume of *Romeo and Juliet*. "Oh, it's beautiful," Adam said as he bent to kiss Beth.

"Read the inscription."

He gently opened the book. "For my friend and truest love." Adam smiled and brushed Beth's mouth

117

lightly with a kiss. He pressed the blue box into her hand.

Nestled on blue velvet was a delicate heart-shaped pendant inscribed "My dearest love."

Beth reached up and gave Adam a big hug. "This is the happiest Christmas of my whole life. You're the best present I could ever have."

Meet the students of Hampstead High . . . students with real-life problems . . . students like you.

Do you know what it's like to be crazy about a boy who doesn't seem to know you're alive? Do you dream of doing something really special, but you're too shy to make your dreams come true? Have you ever had a friendship with a boy turn into something much more?

The girls at Hampstead High know just how you feel! Join Kate, Karen, Beth, and Kim as they discover romance in the world of high school dances, sports, and classes, and make friendships that will change their lives forever.